Little Alpha

By: Krissie Phillips

Little Alpha

Little Alpha

My amazing team.
Mentor: Sherry Foster (Safe haven wolves)
Editor: H. Phillips
Proof reader: Crystal Jackson
Cover Design: Mark Hobbs
desksixtyfour@gmail.com

Little Alpha

Dedication

I'm dedicating this book to my toddler who
became my inspiration for little alpha. He
makes me laugh and he also makes me cry.
We have day to day challenges and this tries
my patience.
He's unruly, stubborn, and master of his
domain, he owns me body and soul.
We have many challenges to come but I
cannot see our lives any other way.
I love you little alpha.

Little Alpha

I may have nearly died of a broken heart but the journey still to come is going to test my survival skills. Not only as a mother but one of a special needs child.

Little Alpha

Prologue

The sudden pain in my chest struck me down like lightening. I couldn't breathe, I couldn't move, I couldn't even scream. The only time a she-wolf feels this sort of pain is when her mate dies. My wolf inside me started howling knowing the impending doom that was to come.

We were going to die. Knowing I didn't have long left finally allowed me to move. Rushing outside to find my alpha, the door came off its hinges.

I had to tell him his beta and best friend was gone before it was too late. Running down the road like a mad woman, pushing past people as I go. Some people asked me what was wrong but I ignored them, with one place in mine I kept running.

Feeling my she-wolf slowly dying inside I finally made it to my alphas house. Without knocking I barge through the door and was met with several pair of eyes.

I didn't know what to say, I didn't know what to do.

If I mentioned to my alpha his beta was dead these unknowns may just challenge him. I tried to take slow deep breaths but that's when the stench greeted my nostrils. The smell of death was all around me. Falling to my knees I begin to whimper.

Suddenly strong arms wrapped around me tenderly and carried me outside.

Looking up I saw it was my alpha; I tried to speak to him however nothing came out.

"I know child be still."

Of course he knew death surrounded me like a cold caress, how could he not know his best friend and beta had died. Running at full speed through our village he took me to his home where many members of our pack surrounded it.

Rushing me inside, he lay me on the lounge. Barking orders at people he looked down at me as my body begun to shake.

My parents came not a moment later followed by our village life witch. I tried to stand and address them but my strength was lagging. I tried reaching out to my mum however I could not.

My wolf must have reached out to hers because she rushed to my side and grabbed my hand. Looking up at my mother there was a millions things I wanted to tell her however I could not, all I could do was lay and slowly die.

The life witch came towards me and began waving her glowing hands over my body. When she gasped everyone looked at her. I knew all was lost, as I felt my wolf tell me her final goodbyes I closed my eyes and waited.

 I could hear the whispers of my pack however I didn't care. Suddenly strong arms grabbed me around the shoulders and began shaking me to death. Popping my eyes open I see it was no other than my alpha.

I could see his lips moving but I couldn't hear a thing he was saying, a sudden slap to my face came out of nowhere.

I finally opened my mouth and a piercing scream came out. Looking around to find who'd done it my mother stepped forward.

"Listen to your alpha!"

Looking back towards him I could see happy tears however there was a look of dread.

"What is it? Why can't I go in peace?"

"You're with child."

"That's not possible my wolf would have known."

"Talk to her please I beg you."

"Why don't you command her?"

"I cannot she's willing herself to die."

Closing my eyes I try to find my wolf in my mind. When I finally found her she was in a tiny ball. Coaching her out was quite difficult however when I was finally able to I opened my mouth.

"Is it true, are we with child?"

She looked at me with sad eyes and nodded her head. My entire world spun on its axis. I was about to die and my child along with me. Opening my eyes I was in a panic. Adrenaline coursed through my veins allowing me to wash away the cold feeling of death.

Placing my hand over my stomach I looked up at my alpha and then my mother. A single tear ran down my cheek. So few wolves in our history survived the death of their mate, I doubted I was anything special. Closing my eyes I wept silently.

A buzzing started up in my mind and my she-wolf lifted her head to take notice. I thought it was finally the end however there was a bright light and my alphas voice penetrated my mind.

"I Jaxson Mills of the Redwater pack command you to live."

I would have laughed except I felt my wolf take notice.

"Amanda it's up to you now, convince her to live if not for you then for your mate's unborn child."

In my mind I opened the connection to my wolf right up and began to beg. It was like a game of tug-of-war. When she pushed I pushed back.

On and on it went until her shaking finally stopped and she curled back into a ball. I tried one my time pleading for her to rise. All she did was look at me with sad broken eyes. I was going to give up when she finally spoke.

"I don't know how to be a mother."

"I know me either however if we die now we will never know."

"I'm so tired."

I was starting to lose her again.

"What do you think Alexander would do?" she thought about it for a moment.

"He would want to fight."

"Exactly, fight with me now."

She looked at me for a sad long moment. Looking down on her paws she huffed out and with one shaky leg at a time finally stood.

"We must leave this place."

I would have agreed with her however the darkness took us away.

Being between life and death is surreal your neither here nor there. It is not hot but it is not cold either. My she-wolf and I stayed like that for what seemed like forever.

After a while we could hear whispers in the darkness, we tried to make sense of it all but neither of us could. Over time those voices started getting louder.

Letting out a groan I hadn't realized I let it out loudly. I felt someone's hands on me and I managed to open my eyes.

Looking around I found myself surrounded by my family and friends. Sighing I tried to

sit up in bed but a hand held me down.
Looking up it was my alpha. I tried to speak
but my mouth felt like I swallowed sand.
My mum came rushing forward with a straw
and a cup of water. I swallowed as fast as I
could so I could find out what was going on.
When the cup was empty I finally spoke.
"What happened? Where are we?"
"I carried you here. After you past out I felt
the best place for you to recover or pass was
your own home."
Looking around I could see all of my things
and my she-wolf and pack howled in pain at
the loss. My wolf noticed a photo of us and
our mate. I began to ball my eyes out. The
reality hit that my she-wolf and I would no
longer have my mate in our lives.
We may have just survived death but our
mate had not. My mum rushed towards me
and jumped onto the bed placing me in her
arms. We stayed like that for several
minutes.
When I was finally done I spoke to my
alpha.
"I have to leave this place."
"Rest for now and we'll sort out new
accommodation later."
"No, I mean our village; I cannot stay here
without my mate."
"You cannot leave if I'm challenged before I
get a new beta…"

"I'm sorry you are no longer my alpha."

"What are you saying?"

"What I'm saying is I Amanda mate to the previous beta of this pack renounce my heritage and claim to this pack."

All was quiet in the room when suddenly several howls broke out around the house. I may regret it later but for now it must be done.

I got out of the bed with shaky legs and held my head high showing my neck in submission.

"I Amanda a lone wolf am asking you Jaxson of the Redwater pack to stay on your lands until your beta my mate is buried within his family plot."

My ex alpha looked at me completely dumbfounded. Not only had I renounced my pack but I was now an outsider asking for permission to stay here and be involved in a packs most secrete moment.

 I could feel the anger and pain washed over him in waves however with a nod of his head he left.

Over the next couple of weeks my parents and old pack members tried to convince me to stay but I knew staying was no good. My she-wolf wouldn't even shift for me so I knew I was making the right choice for all of us.

Little Alpha

When they finally found my mates body we
went through the burial, lifting his soul into
the light and the drunken parade.
I stayed as long as I could until I could stand
it no more. When the time came for the
alpha to pick his new beta I quietly left
under the cover of darkness to hopefully
never return.

Chapter One

Amanda

Living like a human wasn't that bad; I got up, got dressed and went to work like the rest of them. Truth be told I actually didn't have to work however I couldn't just stay at home with my toddler either.

I needed to try and connect with people and allow my child to socialize and have fun until he was able to connect with his wolf. After that I'd have to go into hiding or quite possibly find a new pack.

I was welcome in my old one but I could never go back, not after what happened almost two years ago.

Luckily enough I had several years before his first shift so for now I enjoyed the life we had. After a long shift at the diner I went to grab my toddler and head home. I press the doorbell and waited for one of his carers to answer. When the door opens I place a smile on my face.

"Hi I'm here for Alex."

"Ah yes just a moment and I'll get him."

While I waited for my son a man had shown up and my back stiffened. With just a small intake of breath I realized he was a shifter though my she-wolf wasn't interested in men she did take notice.

17

Letting out a small growl in my mind I stood frozen. Trying not to panic I reached for my she-wolf in my mind but she took no notice of me. After her growl she just curled back into a ball and went to sleep.

This is how she had been since we left the pack. Rarely speaking unless it had to do with our son, we hadn't even shifted in just as long. I smiled kindly at the man but I made no room for interaction.

When my son's teacher finally came I placed him in my arms and rushed out of there without a good-bye.

Hyperventilating I managed to place Alex in his car seat and drove out of there as fast as possible. I hadn't managed to calm down until I was in my home and everything was locked up.

Being a lone wolf was dangerous but being a lone she-wolf well that was a totally different scenario. I could be kidnapped, raped, bred for rouges, killed, you name it. I did the one thing I swore I wouldn't do since I left the pack I called my ex alpha Jaxson.

While I waited for Jaxson to answer I sat on the floor with Alex and tried to calm my breathing. When he finally answered I all but screamed down the phone.

"There was a lone wolf at my day-care today."

"Ah so the male has finally made himself known again. I'll get my team on it and get back to you."

"What do you mean known? Are you telling me there is a rouge roaming around my town?"

"We came across his scent a while ago but he hasn't been back in the territory until recently."

"Well he was at Alex's day-care damn it."

"Amanda you may not be part of the pack anymore but you will respect your tone when talking to an alpha."

"Sorry Jax what am I meant to do I have work tomorrow?"

"Hang on you work?"

"Of course I work."

"Right, well I can have people scouting the area or you can just call in sick."

"I'll call in sick."

"Has he scented you?"

"I don't think so why?"

"If he had scented your she-wolf there would be a need for concern."

"Oh well then we should be fine."

"You're not telling me what I think you're telling me are you?"

"Well Casey hasn't, more like doesn't…"

"Amanda a cooped up wolf isn't safe for anyone you need to force her out."

"Don't you think I've tried? You try losing a part of yourself and then try and shift. Remember if it wasn't for Alex I would be dead."

Hearing his sigh over the phone I was heartbroken. I knew deep down he was right but my wolf was still morning even after two years.

"We'll be fine I'll protect Alex."

I stood in complete and utter shock Casey had opened the connection in my mind to her. Twice in one day was a small victory, it was even better when she spoke to me. Honestly it was like a rush of fresh crisp air to the lungs, how I missed the connection. I felt the power of my wolf surround me like a warm caress.

"Jax are you still there?"

"Yes what happen?"

"Casey talked to me, said she will protect Alex."

"Maybe this is what she needs to come out. As wolves we serve and protect it's in her nature."

"I know that, like hello, been a wolf for like forever!"

"Alright, alright, anyway I'm going to go but if you see or smell him again ring, as of now I'll put scouts out and find out what he's up to."

"Thank you Jax."

For over a week no one had seen, talked to, or smelt this new wolf around the territory or even around town. After a while I thought it was maybe a fluke and decided it was finally time to get out of the house.

Packing Alex's nappy bag I grabbed him up and placed him in his pram. Stepping outside I looked around but I couldn't see anyone around.

Turning to lock the door Casey suddenly took over my body for a split second and smelt the environment around us.

"What is it what's wrong?"

"Nothing I was just checking."

Sighing out in relief I didn't make a big deal out of it as this was third times this week that she has made her presents known. I could feel her in my mind and she was on high alert which made me feel a little twitchy.

For a while everything was quiet except Alex who was babbling in excitement. After a while we came across Alex's favorite hangout the park and he squealed in delight.

"Okay, okay sweetie will go."

Inside my mind I ask Casey if it is safe and she said it was. Pushing the pram over I go around the front and unclasp Alex so he can go and play. Crossing my arms I watch as he goes down all the slides.

Taking out my phone I take photos and videos to send to my mum and dad later. Some mums from Alex's day-care had started to show up and before long we were all chatting and watching our children squeal and play with delight.

"Amanda long time no see."

"Yeah I had a stomach bug, couldn't get out of bed."

"Oh that's terrible."

"Oh I'm fine really Alex was great."

"You're such a good mum to him if I was sick I'd be dead on the floor."

A few of the mums laughed and nodded their heads in agreement. Truth be told I don't know how they believed the lie. Shifters don't get sick like humans.

In the past two years I'd never had a day off work and Alex never missed day-care. Suddenly a scream broke out near the slides. Several of the mums went rushing forwards to see whose kid it was.

I stood shocked at the scene before me Alex's eyes were glowing and the child that had screamed had a huge bite mark on his arm.

Alex had never bitten a child in his life, like why now? Getting into action I Scooped Alex up and turned him away from the group. I went over to the mum whose child had been bitten and apologized profusely.

She just laughed it off and said boys will be boys however I was devastated. This wasn't a case of kids being kids this was a mega wolf problem and I had no alpha to talk to. Apologizing again I went over to the pram and put Alex in it luckily enough his eyes had stopped glowing.

Walking out of there as fast as I could Casey picked up on something which had her making me growl out loud. Completely freaked I run home going this way and that until I felt Casey settle.

Once we got inside I locked all the doors and sunk to the ground.

"Mum, mum, mum."

"Oh shizz sorry buddy hang on."

I got up and took Alex out of the pram and he took off straight to his room. Putting my head between my knees I knew I had to tell Jaxson what happened but I also knew the outcome, my family will come for Alex.

I stayed home another week which Casey was really grateful for, whatever had spooked her at the park had allowed her to keep the connection between us wide open. Finally one night after putting Alex to bed I rung Jax.

"Hi Amanda no we haven't scented the wolf yet."

"I um, err…"

"What is it are you in danger?"

"No but something happened last week."

"Was it the wolf?"

"No but now you mention it I'll talk about that in a minute its um it's got to do with Alex."

"What is it is he alright?"

"Yes, yes his fine but um he kind of bit a human child and his eyes were glowing."

"HIS WHAT?"

"It was an accident."

"Shit, alright you need to command Casey to come out and smell her child NOW!"

"What, what is it, what's wrong?"

"JUST DO IT!"

Putting the phone down I tried to talk to Casey however she was adamant she wouldn't change. What came next I wasn't proud of but if Jax thought something was up I knew to always listen. I got undressed and physically forced the change on us. With my bones cracking and taking on my she-wolf form I whimpered in pain. Since leaving the pack I hadn't transformed or forced Casey to transform which I was now paying the price for.

Finally on all fours I made my way to my son's room and suddenly smelt a wolf. Pouncing in I looked everywhere but couldn't find anyone in my son's room. Going over to Alex I nudged him with my nose. Casey let out a sudden growl. My son had a wolf's scene all over him. I tried to transform back but Casey wouldn't allow it. She took charge and ran all through the house looking for this wolf. After finding nothing we went back to the phone and Casey laid down on our paws and whimpered.

"Casey you need to give me back Amanda." She looked at the phone and turned our head to the side. Whimpering again she got up and nudged the phone. She let out a yip and licked it. If I hadn't been in distress I would have laughed   at her antics she was actually missing our old alpha.

"It's okay we'll go see everyone soon just let me talk to Jax."

She lowered her head in submission and allowed me to talk control and transform. When I was me again I put the phone on speaker and got dressed.

"Jax a wolf has been here but I don't recognize it."

"Was the smell around Alex or the rest of the house?"

Sitting on the lounge I tried to remember. There was a faint smell in both the bathroom and lounge however the distinct smell just came off Alex.

"There was a faint smell in some of the rooms but it was mostly all over Alex."

"Okay don't be alarmed but your son is an alpha's alpha."

"HE'S A WHAT?"

"I said don't be alarmed."

"Of course I'm going to be alarmed they're wolves of legend and bedtime stories. If it's true he's going to change much sooner than I had planned for. How is this even possible his father was only a beta?"

"Well that isn't exactly true."

"What are you saying Jax."

"What I'm saying is Alexander was meant to be alpha before you were born."

"What the hell why wasn't I told this?"

"Amanda now is not the time. I need to know have you got somewhere you can go."

"Yes my cabin up in the woods just outside your borders."

"Good, good and now about the bite."

"Oh god no more bad news please."

"I'm sorry but this is an alpha secret past from alpha to alpha."

"Why are you telling me?"

"Because you're Alex's mother, Alex has chosen his beta."

"HE'S DONE WHAT? He's not even two yet."

"I know, I know, calm down it normally doesn't happen like this but your wolves without a pack his wolf made its choice, now we have to deal with it."

"How is that even possible?"

"I don't have the time to explain everything, right now you need to find that other child's mother and get them away from town before Alex's birthday. If we're lucky that child has also bitten his mum and she won't freak out too much."

"Jax you're talking about possible kidnapping."

"No just quietly coaching her out of town just in time for their first shift."

"How am I meant to do that? Oh hi remember me the mum who's child bit your child and now his a wolf... follow me."

"Yeah I see your point. Look I will deal with the mum you just get Alex to the cabin."

"Alright."

Hanging up the phone I close my eyes and look for Casey in my mind.

"You forgot to tell him about the other thing at the park."

"Don't you think we have bigger problems right now?"

"You are right what are we going to do?"

"I don't know Casey I really don't know."

Surprising the hell out of me she pushed forth in my mind and made her first shift in two years. I didn't know what to say or do so I just watched to see what she would do. She ended up walking into Alex's room and jumped on his bed. Curling into a ball she surprisingly went to sleep. Thinking about her behavior had two things going through my mind before she went to sleep.

The first was she has chosen her new alpha and the second she was being over protective which meant I would see more of her. That night I had the best night's sleep in a very long time as I knew Casey was on watch.

The next morning I woke up to a scream of joy. Casey jump out of bed on high alert and looked around. Nothing was out of place but Alex was gone. She went to turn around but two little tiny hands grabbed us around our neck.

"PUPPY!"

Dear god no, I was no damn puppy. Casey let out what her version of a laugh was which caused Alex to look alarmed making his eyes glow. Casey automatically put her head up in submission. Gleefully this indulged my son causing him to clap and squeal. Great just bloody great not like my son didn't own me already, now Casey had a new alpha that was not even two years old yet. This was going to be hell.

Chapter Two

Amanda

Over the next couple of weeks I dropped our whole lives and tried everything within my power to get to know this other mum. However with Alex's birthday quickly approaching I was running out of time, I didn't have a choice but to up and leave town. Grabbing everything I could I put the house on the market and left. In a day or two a removalist was going to bring the rest of our things.

Driving up the windy road to the cabin Alex started to become unsettled. Lately it was a normal occurrence due to his wolf reaching out. As I was about to go around a turn Alex let out an ear piercing squeal which made Casey rush to the front of my mind.

Pushing out my will for control I managed to but not before the car had spun out of control. Turning the wheel I put my foot on the brake but it was of no use.

The car went spinning into a ditch and became stuck.

Breathing heavily I turn in my seat to check Alex. His eyes where glowing which made Casey whimper. My son's wolf was powerful indeed. Though I had my ex

mate's strength due to our mating my power
was weak in comparison.

Seeing that Alex was okay I managed to get
out of the car. Heavily breathing I grabbed
my phone from my pocket and dialed
Jaxson, whatever was happening to my son
was not natural. Luckily he picked up on the
third ring.

"Jax it's me Amanda."

"Have you made it to the cabin yet?"

"Not exactly."

"What do you mean?"

"Alex's wolf's power did something causing
Casey to react causing us to crash."

"Shit are you both alright?"

"Yes, we're fine but what the hell is going
on. Power is rolling off him."

"I'm coming just get to the cabin."

He hung up on me and I just stared at my
phone. What the hell was going on with my
child? Was this alpha's alpha stuff really
true? Putting my phone back in my pocket I
went behind the car and started pushing.
Thanks to my shifter strength I had it out of
the ditch in no time at all. After that I
reached into my nappy bag and grabbed
drinks, snacks and videos, everything and
anything to try and make the rest of the trip
in one piece.

Jumping back in the car I turned the key
however for a while nothing happened.

Begging, pleading and saying a million curse words in my head the car finally started. Driving as fast but as safe as I could I managed to get to the cabin an hour later unharmed.

Opening all the doors of the car I went around the back and got the play pen out and headed to the cabin. Once unlocked I walked inside and set the pen up in the lounge room. Going out to the car I got Alex out followed by the snacks, drinks and movies.

Going inside I place him in the pen and put a movie in the DVD player. Once I see Alex is completely relaxed I head out to the car and grab everything else. By the time I was done I was exhausted however I needed to get ready for Jaxson and hopefully my son's soon to be beta's arrival.

While Alex watched his movie I locked the door and removed the pen from around him. I went about moving furniture around to make play room and I took all the plastic covers of the furniture and sprayed them down.

Afterward I opened all the windows and went into the kitchen and unpacked all the food. It looked like I had a months' worth but alpha's and beta's needed a lot of nutrients' plus I may also have another female wolf to entertain.

Once everything was set I went to sit down
on the chair but a knock at the door had me
bouncing back up.

Casey came forth in my mind however once
she scented the new comer she wagged her
tail and relaxed. Opening the door I found
Jax on the other side. Unable to hold back
the emotional flood gates I crashed straight
into his chest and wrapped my hands around
his neck.

A slight growl came from the lounge room.
Turning my head I see Alex's eyes were
glowing and he was watching us quite
intently.

I let Jax go but not before I felt a shudder
run over his body. Looking him in the face
with a raised eyebrow I waited but he just
shook his head. Getting the hint I walked
into the lounge room and got Jax to sit as far
away from us as possible.

No one said anything for a while as we were
waiting to see what Alex would do.

Eventually not seeing Jax as a threat he
walked over to me and jumped in my lap to
continue his movie.

"His power is incredible I've only witnessed
it a few times in my life."

"What does it all mean?"

"Not now I swear I'll explain it all but for
now we must get ready for guests."

"Oh, who's coming?"

"Let's just say you're no longer alone in this."

After that Jax updated me on my parents and the pack. I nodded along however I couldn't get into the conversation so it eventually died out and we all sat in silence. Just before nightfall another knock came at the door. Looking at Jax he said it was some of the pack and a guest. Going over I open the door and a toddler comes flying past me.

Looking back up to see who was there was an emotional roller-coaster. My parents were there alongside a man I assumed was Jax's beta and the mother of the child my son bit. Unable to say anything I just moved aside and allowed everyone to come inside.

Once everyone was inside and seated I went about getting drinks and food for everyone. Jax followed me into the kitchen and helped with everything, however every time I asked a question he just shut me down with a shake of the head.

When everyone had a drink and a small plate of sandwiches and snacks did the conversation finally pick up.

"So did everyone get here okay?"

Everyone stated yes and then my parents questioned both me and my son's betas mother who I found   out was called Melissa. Everyone casually talked and there were a few giggles from my folks but you could just feel the tension in the air. Both the toddlers seemed to be getting along okay until a scream went up in the room. A chair went clattering to the floor. Looking over it was Melissa who was backing away from us.

Without saying a word my parents scooped up both the boys and took them away.

Turning to Jax he just shrugged. It looked like I was in this on my own.

"Are you okay Melissa?"

"I, I, I… Their eyes."

"It's okay love remember we said this might happen."

Looking between the strange man and Melissa I waited and then the unbelievable happened she ran straight into his arms. My Jaw completely dropped to the floor. Jax looked between us all and let out a laugh. Getting up from my chair I went around to Jax and punched him quite hard in the shoulder. This just caused another bout of laughter and I stormed outside.

It looked like I was out of the loop with everything, even Casey wasn't impressed. Sitting down on the step I took slow deep breaths. I was in a world of hurt and confusion; all this was just too much. After a while Jax came outside however he walked pass me and stood in the front yard.

"So are you going to explain?"

"Which part?"

"Are you friggen kidding me Jax the whole dam thing."

"Well after you tried and failed with Melissa I sent ever single male pack member to tail her."

"So how did that happen?"

"Well Simon was one of the last to go as he was my beta after you know."

I just nodded my head in agreement. I didn't need my mate mentioned right now. Casey however growled in my mind for her Jax having a beta was a betrayal to Alexander. I just shook my head and waited.

"Anyway little Michael in there had bit his mum and awoke the power in her. Simon losing his head followed her home and barged down her door."

"Oh my god you can't be serious."

"Dead serious she pepper sprayed him and then grabbed Michael and took off."

It wasn't funny but this story had me in stitches it's been a known fact males tend to do crazy, funny and sometimes dangerous things to get to their mate. Once a male senses his mate well it's all about the cock after that. After I finished laughing Jax continued.

"So anyway after I beat his arse senseless I made him chase her all over town."

"You did not."

This story was just getting better and better. "Well he needed to find her and apologize for his stupidity, However with some help she bumped place to place till I finally stepped in and told her what the hell was going on."

"How did she take that?"

"I freaked the fuck out what do you think I did."

Turning around I see Simon and Melissa come out hand in hand. Looking at Simon's face he was bright red. I couldn't wait for the rest.

"Anyway she freaked out so Simon came to the rescue. His wolf however got too excited and came forth and well…"

"Well what?"

"He pissed himself like full blown over the top excited to the point he peed."

That was it I completely lost it. I was rolling around on the steps. After a while I pulled myself together but looking at Melissa I just started laughing again. Simon let out a growl obviously embarrassed but that set off two sets of growls inside. Looking at Jax we bolted inside.

Going through the house we found my parents with the boys in the bathroom. My parents were almost pushed up against the wall due to the boys; their combined power was making all the wolves crazy.

"Holy shit what do we do."

"I, I don't know."

Melissa stepped into the room and without thinking she grabbed her son. My son saw it as a threat and eyed her off causing Melissa to whimper.

"Alex ENOUGH."

He turned his head to me however instead of seeing glowing eye's I just got his baby blues. Going over I   grabbed him up and turned him away from everyone. My parents relaxed instantly and I turned to Jax.

"We need help."

"We can't."

"Why not?"

"I'll explain everything after the boys get put to bed."

Nodding my head I went into the lounge room where I dressed and gave Alex his dummy for bed. Grabbing his tiny little hand I walked him down the hallway to the room I was putting the boys in but decided better of it and put him in my room. Putting on the night light and his soft music I kissed him goodnight and left the room. Once I closed the door I was greeted by Melissa in the hallway.

"I am so sorry you're caught in this mess."

"It's okay really I have Simon so."

I nodded my head however my body
retaliated with a wave of grief. It caused
both Melissa and I to whimper.
"I'm so sorry."
"It's okay I'm not really alone you're all
here."
Melissa grabbed my hand.
"We're not going anywhere… what's the
term I'm looking for, ah yes we're pack."
I squeezed her hand and showed her two
rooms which she could use, however like me
she stuck Michael in with her.
"What about Simon?"
"Oh he can have the lounge."
"But he's your mate."
"Oh he hasn't claimed me yet."
"Why not?"
"He scared the crap out of me."
"Oh so the dog box then."
We both giggle and hear laughter and a
growl from the lounge room. Leaving
Melissa to get Michael settled I head into the
lounge where my mum gets up and opens
her arms. Stepping into them I let it all out.
The grief, the frustration, the confusion just
everything. After a while my tears stop and I
step away from my mum.
"It's all going to be okay."
"How?"

"We're all going to help you, both of you. You see Simon myself and your father renounced our claim to the pack."
I looked at my mother and then my father who smiled and nodded his head.
"But why, you guys love the pack. You cannot leave."
"Honestly a change feels like what we need and honestly we want to help."
"But no one can help."
"Actually Amanda that's not true there is one person."
"Really who?"
"Our regional Alpha."
"Our who?"
"As you know every pack is run by an alpha but who do you think we answer too?"
"I figured yourself." He laughed and shook his head.
"Not exactly there is a council full of the most powerful wolf shifters known only to us normal alphas."
"So what do they do?"
"They keep the peace."
"And?"
"I'm not sure I'm not one but I know if I reach out our regional will come."
"And you think Alex is one of these wolves."
"Yes I've met one before."
"So all the stories?"

"Are true I just don't know how much, it's their secret information."

"Why haven't you gotten a hold of him then?"

"Well that's the thing ours is missing."

"What do you mean by that?"

"I mean he's just gone."

"So what the hell are we to do Alex is two tomorrow."

"I, I don't know I'm trying other packs to see if they can contact theirs."

"So there is hope?"

"I honestly don't know."

That night I went to bed but I could not sleep. Casey was stir crazy as there were wolves here without a pack making the surroundings dangerous to her. The only thing that stopped her jumping out of my skin was knowing that they were family and in time they would be pack. Sometime around dawn I managed to shut my eyes but it was too late. Alex jumped on me wanting his morning milk and his breakfast. Grabbing him in a bear hug I smothered him is kisses and wished him a happy birthday. For the most part the day was uneventful. Just your normal cake and presents, however as the day drew on everyone began to be on high alert. As soon as the moon rose three people's lives were going to change forever. Jax, my parents,

Simon and myself had all been through the change before so the moon didn't affect us but watching and waiting was killing us. At exactly 7:05 P.M the moon was high enough and that's when the first whimper happened. Simon rushed over to Melissa. Being her first change it was going to hurt like hell. He took her outside and as far away from the boys as he could.

As for the rest of us we just watched and waited but nothing happened. Everyone was looking completely dumbfounded. The boys were just that, two naked little boys running around my lounge room. After a while I put clothes on the boys and everyone begun to relax.

"I don't get it what happened?"

"I have no clue Melissa is…"

"I know that's the thing she's changing as we speak but the boys."

"I don't know."

Suddenly my front door got knocked into my house and the biggest wolf I have ever seen walked in. Jax, mum and dad turned instantly to face the intruder however I went to grab the boys. When I reached the boys the weirdest transformation of my life happened. One second they were boys the next they were tiny balls of fluff. I literally had no time to feel anything because the two

tiny little fluff balls decided to take on the
wolf at my door.
Pushing Casey forward in my mind I
jumped over the boys losing my clothes in
the process. In my she-wolf form I turned on
the pom pom's and growled. The boys sat
and wagged their cute little tails. Barking at
the others they ushered the boys back.
Turning back to the intruder I lean down in a
defensive stance and growled, however
another friggen weird thing happened, the
big bad wolf was lying on the floor with his
legs up in the air and a freaky grin on its
face. Great just great.

Chapter Three

Lachlan

When my brother died I became nothing more than a broken man, honor and duty were top priority. It was us and a few others on the council. We each had become each other's family. Before his death he told me another was born. I knew what that meant I had to find this child and bring him to the council to be raised in our ways.

Did I feel for the unexpected mother yes of course but what had to be done was for the sake of wolf shifters everywhere. If left to their own devices a greater alpha could be dangerous and in rare cases had to be put down by the supreme council.

I searched many shifter territories over the last two years but I came up empty.

It wasn't until I came across a small town in my brother's region that my wolf noticed something was different. I went near a shifter territory however I couldn't place the child. Covering my actual scent I allowed them to chase me off thinking I was a lone wolf however I hung around.

In my human form I took up my job as a child educator and scouted all the schools and childcare centers.

I didn't need a job but the position allowed me to get close to the children and take them without causing a pack riot. To shifters, children are priceless so without listening they will die to keep the child safe.

I was heading into the last childcare center in the town when I got a slight whiff of a wolf. Standing before me was a female and my wolf became curious. Taking a big whiff I noticed nothing.

If it wasn't her then it had to be one of the workers. She smiled at me and almost stepped back. When the door opened I was hit with power. I tried making sense of all the people and smells but this little alpha was everywhere. The mother grabbed her child and took off rather quickly. Turning back to the educator I put on my award winning smile and introduced myself.

When she allowed me access to the center I walked around and tried to be interested in what she was saying; however it was just the same as the other places I had been. I allowed my wolf to come forth and smell all the children that were left and also the workers.

The child wasn't here and no female here was a wolf. I told the woman I'd be back tomorrow to access all the children, she gave me a smiled and let me go.

I know I'm an old wolf but my nose has never been wrong a she-wolf and a greater alpha wolf had been there of that I was certain. Over the next week the smell died down and by the end of it I was thinking I was just imagining things.

Maybe I had just hoped to get it over with; my hopes were just too high. On the way to my hotel I came across a park where some mothers and their children were playing. Suddenly I was hit with a magical force and I heard a child scream.

Being a lone male I knew I couldn't just walk into the group and grab a child so I left in the hope to find him or her another way. Greater alpha babies' power came in waves so it was just a matter of feeling and seeking.

For a while I lost track of the child however the power had me running all over town, this child felt like it was everywhere and then nowhere at the same time.

I was going to call in reinforcements but I decided to do another scouting trip of the territory and town. Again I came across nothing but high up in the mountains that changed. I smelt a very scared female and low and behold the little greater alpha. Following the scent I came to a ditch where it seems a car had gone off the road.

Here the area reeked of both the terrified female and the greater alpha; following the trail for a while I came across a lone cabin. Hiding in the bushes I watched the little house for a while but no one came or went. I thought about going up for a closer look however a few cars came rushing up the drive way. Watching as everyone got out of the cars I smelt one wolf I dreaded to smell.

This territories alpha was here. Not knowing what to do I just watched and waited. Surprisingly nothing came of that night so I had a nap and was woken by squealing children. Looking up from my hiding spot I saw several people watching and playing with two toddlers.

I had finally found him!

I was going to come out of my hiding place but guilt ripped through my body. Watching how happy this family was to be together I just felt like the mother needed more time.

So as the hours crept by I just waited silently. The only noise that came from the house was a scream and a female and the alpha came outside.

As I listened to their conversation I couldn't help but laugh, however I felt for the other female. Tonight she would turn and every bone would break in her body.

It was all my fault if only I had gotten here sooner. Eventually night had fallen and I heard a whimper in the house. A male and the female came rushing out running into the trees. I stayed where I was however as time went on nothing else seemed to happened.

Having had enough I rush to the house and force the door in. I was greeted by an elderly couple and the alpha which had all transformed. The female scared for the children ran towards them, however in my presence they both transformed into little wolves. Coming towards me they both growled and were defending their family. However what shocked me most was the female jumped over them transforming mid-air.

This situation was getting more complicated by the second. An alpha and a betas mate, what the hell was I going to do? Thinking I may just retreat I watch as the she-wolf growled at the pups and barked at the others to guard the children. Just as she was turning a different kind of magic hit me and it was the kind that someone like me was not meant to have. Before I knew it I was belly up with my tongue hanging out of my head.

I had lost all control of my body and boy was I pissed. A million thoughts ran through my mind and were stressing me out, not to mention right now I just wanted to shift out of this wolf to kick its arse. The she-wolf looked at me with many emotions but she tried to hide the worst of them.

My wolf sent out the claim and she just sat on her butt with her tail wagging. If I didn't get off this floor soon I was going to look like a complete fool. What was worse was I had a mate and I was trying to take her baby. This night just gets better and better.

"Cade we have to get off the floor."

"Why she is our mate."

"Because we look ridiculous."

"But she is our mate I want her."

"We cannot have a mate."

"Why not she is pretty."

"She will also want to rip our face off when I tell her why we're here."

"We cannot take the pups."

"We have to it is what is done."

"NO I will refuse to change."

"You cannot do that.

"Well I'll bring the pups back."

"You will do no such thing."

"Can't you see our mate hurts? Taking the pups might kill her."

"She's better off without all of us."

"No she won't."

Sighing my wolf realized I wasn't giving in but I wasn't exactly saying yes either. In my confused state he allowed me to sit up causing the female alarm. Rushing forward my wolf pushed us to the floor lying on our belly in submission. Nothing happened for a while; however the reason I came here came bouncing toward me, the two balls of fluff.

The other wolves had lost control of the pups and the greater alpha was feeling his mother's pain. He came rushing at me and bit my foot. I tried to growl however my wolf leaned down and bumped him with our nose. The female growled and then transformed. Looking at her closely it was the female from the childcare center.

I was in total shock. I had in fact smelt her and she was no wolf. All I could think of was maybe the greater alpha had been adopted or another in the pack gave birth and he bit her. Needing answers and feeling like I had to give answers of my own I pressured my wolf into transforming.

Though my wolf was going berserk in my mind he eventually allowed us to transform back. I excused myself and went to retrieve my clothing. When I was dressed I walked back to the house, I actually knocked on the door frame this time. The female walked over with her hands on her hips and just glared at me.

"I um, um I'll pay to get that fixed."

"Or you can tell us who the bloody hell you are!"

"That's a regional alpha. But how?"

"You've got to be kidding me."

"Your alpha's right, can I come in and I'll explain everything."

"Like I have a choice."

She stormed off in a huff; I however put the door sort of back in the frame so the pups couldn't escape. Turning back around the female had sat down with her arms crossed glaring at me. Unsure what to do or what to say I just watched the pups play.

"Begging your pardon regional but how are you here?"

"My brother died two years ago to the day I've been searching out his replacement."

"His replacement?"

"Yes when one of us dies it means a new as you say regional wolf is born."

"So you haven't come to help us?"

"I um… In a way."

"You mean…"

"I've come to take the pup however seeing he has a beta I have no choice but to take them both."

A howl enraptured from outside and two wolves came barreling inside their hackles raised and ready for battle. The female inside had also joined them but seemed to be in a battle of wills with her wolf. No one moved for a moment until the alpha spoke out.

"Everyone relax I'm sure we can come up with an agreement?"

"Not likely alpha the children must come for their safety and yours."

"But they haven't hurt anyone."

"And yet the little alpha has bitten a child my guess a human one in turn biting and turning the female behind me. Am I correct?"

"I um well I guess but it was an accident."

"It may have been but as they get older the more wild if not feral they become it's dangerous for wolves and humans alike."

"Please I beg you, you just can't she will…"

The female in front of me turned her head and growled at her alpha which shut him up. This situation was getting more interesting by the minute. I cautiously took several steps and sat on one of the chairs. I seriously needed to find a way to make these people see sense, their children were a danger. If it wasn't for my wolves' threat I'd have just taken them and run.

"Alpha I have some questions of my own?"

"Alright but this conversation isn't over."

"I agree for now. Why can't you control your pack members? What sort of pack are you running here?"

"I um well none of these people are in my pack."

"So why are you here?"

"I…"

"He and the rest are here for me and our toddlers." The female had transformed and had placed her hands on her hips. Nudity for shifters was rather common however just looking at this female had my dick going hard instantly. Needing   to adjust myself I swiftly moved however the female saw the movement and sneered.

"Look I'll level with you all, this situation has gotten beyond complicated so why don't we all just sit down and talk about it?"

"Oh so we can all become besties and then you take off with our children when our backs are turned. No thanks."

"Please you're making my wolf rather distressed."

"Oh and you haven't ours… YOU JUST SAID YOU'RE TAKING OUR CHILDREN!"

"I well um I'd say call it even but you look like you want to bite me."

"I'll do more than bite."

"Oh I hope so."

"Keep dreaming I'll renounce your claim."

As soon as she said that she dropped to her knees holding and shaking her head.

"What's the matter with her?"

I got up in a panic and went to help but the wolves behind me came past me building a wall of fur and snarls.

"Tell them to let me past; if I command them everyone here will fall. I don't want to hurt the children."

"I, I, I cannot I already told you they're not pack not since Alex."

Speaking of the little one he bounced over into his mother's lap and was whining. The female place a hand around him and pulled him close. Leaning to his ear she whispered though I could hear it.

"You saved me once, save me again."

What did she mean again? After a while the female fought through the pain; however she sat on a chair with the little alpha on her lap.

"Are you alright?"

"Just dandy if you want to talk start otherwise leave."

"You know I can't"

"Well there it's six of us and one of you so."

"Your odds are void I am the oldest and strongest left on the council besides I will not willingly kill a possible mate."

"Aha possible my arse, not happening."

"I cannot agree or disagree for I must talk to the other council members."

"So regional what do we do? They will fight, you won't fight, what are our options?"

"Honestly I don't know."

The female hugged her pup tight a slow stream of tears running down her face. It was taking everything in me to not go to her and tell her it was all going to be alright because in reality it may just not be. Everyone sat quietly for a moment and a few of the others surrounded the female.

My wolf was whimpering in my mind but I had no soothing words. In the end I decided to leave but told them I'd come back tomorrow and we would try and figure out something then. Getting undressed on the front lawn I transform back into my wolf and let the others be. Hiding in the bushes I saw everyone come outside after a while and allow the little pups some fresh air. What would it be like to live a simple kind of life?

"We can have that you know."

"You know we can't it isn't done."

"Who said?"

"It's been the law since forever."

"Maybe it's time for a change."

"And if something was to happen? War, outbreaks, rouges?"

"With us here we won't let that happen."

My wolf curled up in a ball and went to sleep leaving no room for debate. This left me pondering the situation at hand. Could we really change things? And what of the female she was a puzzle indeed. Smiling at the picture of her naked in my mind I fell asleep starring into those stormy eyes.

Chapter Four

Amanda

After that mongrel left it left Casey with her fur in a twist and I was seriously none too pleased.

"We could use another mate again."

"No we don't."

"But he might be good for us."

"Have you seriously forgotten everything that has happened?"

"Of course not."

"Well then we don't need to discuss this further."

"But I'm so lonely."

"Well you wouldn't have been if you had just let me in."

"I know but…"

"No buts… After Alexander just no."

"But…"

"NO BUTS we nearly died and did you forget that he wants to take the children away."

"Of course not but he won't his wolf won't allow it."

"Yeah well we'll see. Come one let's take the pups outside."

Shutting the connection to Casey I scooped up Alex and told everyone to take the kids outside. When we got out there I looked around but all in all it seemed the alpha had disappeared. I wasn't a fool though I knew he was sitting there bidding his time. Putting Alex down I allowed him to run around the front yard under the moon light.

"So what are we going to do darling?"

"Honestly mum I don't know."

Sighing I just continued to watch the pups. Eventually Casey wanted to join them and that's exactly what I did.

Shedding my clothes I allowed her to take over and once in wolf form I went and lay down on the grass. The pups come over eagerly and started chewing on my paws and trying to lick my face. Nudging them away with my nose ended up causing them to pounce excitedly all over me.

This game went on for a while and before long everyone joined in. Everyone in wolf form happily played with the pups till the light of dawn and then we all went inside for a sleep.

A few hours later I got up and it was lunch time, I checked on the boys both of them had managed to wreak havoc in the room. Pillows were destroyed, blankets everywhere torn or shredded. Among the mayhem two little naked toddlers slept happily.

Going into the kitchen I found Jaxson making coffee. He gave me a cup which I took greedily. It was a huge twenty four hours and the caffeine was exactly what I needed to get my brain ticking.

"So how are you feeling?"

"I'm fine, tired. Raising pups wasn't exactly how I saw my life you know."

He nodded his head and stirred his coffee without actually looking at it.

"I came up with an idea but it is highly dangerous."

"What will it do to the children?"

"Nothing I hope but if he tries to take the kids..."

"Right well spit it out."

"Well if what he said is true and they take children I was thinking of getting the pack involved and if possible the nearby packs."

"Wont that draw too much attention?"

"It might but the more people here the more likely they will leave us alone. Besides who doesn't love a good party?"

"Where would everyone stay? How will they be able to transform?"

"Don't you worry about that? I'll figure everything out. You just keep those pups safe. You might not be pack but your family even if the laws say you aren't."

Nodding my head I had to turn away because I had tears in my eyes. This really showed me things could change however would this cause chaos or would everything be okay? Going outside to sit down to enjoy my coffee the alpha from yesterday walked over.

"Sorry to intrude however we do need to talk."

"We do but you're not going inside."

"That's understandable can I at least get one of those."

Saying nothing I just stared at him however Jaxson came out with a fresh mug and handed it over. He nodded his head and walked back inside.

"Mmmm just the way I like it."

"How did he know to do that?"

"Being a greater alpha we can communicate with all wolves however in human form we can only talk to the alphas."

"Being a what?"

"Greater alpha, it's what we call ourselves as our powers are greater than the average alpha."

"Rightio."

"So I do have a question for you."

"Oh really."

"More curiosity really but how were you able to hide your wolves scent from me. I should have picked up that you were a wolf straight away?"

"I don't know I mean I haven't really had a wolf till recently."

"So the boy did change you?"

"No I've been a wolf my whole life however after…"

"After what?"

I couldn't help but sigh even though it had been two years the pain still ran deep.

"My mate Jaxson's previous beta he well… he died. I nearly died too however I managed to survive for Alex's sake."

"That doesn't explain how you covered your scent, only greater alphas can."

"Well Casey took the loss harder and disappeared we hadn't transformed or really communicated since   then."

"I'm sorry for your loss but it still doesn't explain the scent."

"I don't know maybe Alex gave me some of his power."

"Maybe."

"So are you going to take the children?"

"Honestly I don't know."

"Well good luck on what you decide."

"What do you mean?"

"We're not taking this laying down without a fight!"

"Yes I heard your conversation with your old alpha."

"So you think it's dumb?"

"What, no, I just can't promise anything, there are rules we need to live by."
"I'll take you to the supreme shifter council."
"Aha that's funny."
"Why is that?"
"Wolves haven't dealt with the supreme shifter council for a long time."
"Well I don't know but you're not taking the children I'd die before that happens."
A growl erupted for his month and I just looked at him with a raised eyebrow.
"I um sorry… just don't talk about dying my wolf doesn't like it."
"Well your wolf is your issue not mine."
Having said that he let out another growl and Casey whimpered within my mind however I ignore them both.
"Look I have to go but for now just be careful."
"About time."
This time both wolves made us growl and surprisingly we both laughed. He put the coffee cup down and stared at me for a few moments and then turned to leave.
"Oh before I forget just so you know, Alex's wolf will mature quickly which in turn will allow him to claim a pack. For greater alphas it's uncommon now but it use to happen a lot. I suggest if his wolf reaches out do it".

Nodding my head I watched him leave. I walk inside and everyone was up including the children.

"So I guess you all heard that?"

"Indeed what are you going to do?"

Well Casey by the looks of things has already made up our mind. She has treated Alex like our Alpha since she realized he was different. I guess we just sit back and wait. I'm not going to lie this looks like it could get dangerous. I recommend you all go back to the pack. Obviously Melissa and Simon wont but mum and dad please."

"Oh honey Jaxson already told us what's going to go down, we got you."

"Thanks mum."

I walked up to her and wrapped myself in her embrace. I was glad I wasn't doing this alone, having my family around I may just get through this.

"I must say Amanda Alex's wolf is aging quite fast. Being a greater alpha has allowed me to open a   connection to him."

"Oh so soon."

"Indeed it's quite fascinating. Alex will be a handful indeed but with a maturing wolf and with my help I think you will be fine. I however suggest you all move to pack lands until we figure this mess out."

"For once I'll agree with you."

Everyone else nodded their heads and we began to pack everything up. When everything was done we all got in the cars however Jaxson got in with us to avoid any mishaps like what happened when we first got here.

It was a nice easy journey and before long we were in pack territory. Following Jaxson's instructions I drove to the back of the territory were several new houses had been built.

Getting out of the car I grabbed Alex and I took him to the middle house. Jaxson said it was for our protection as the others will surround us. It seemed Jaxson had been busy in the last few years.

The pack housing had dramatically grown. Soon enough he would have to expand his lands so as to actually make this a proper community. Walking into the house I put Alex down and allowed him to toddle off.

"I'm going to have a pack meeting and let them know what's going on. I'll be back as soon as I can."

"Jax I'm so sorry."

"You have nothing to be sorry for its just life."

He smiled and walked out the door. Looking around the house it was a simple set up, three rooms, bath, shower, and kitchen. It reminded me of the set up I had at home.

My mood dramatically dropped as that wasn't home any more. In fact I had no home to speak of and this was just temporary. Sitting down I place my elbows on my knees and my head in my hands. What was a mother to do?

In the end I found one of the rooms and grabbing a dummy I laid down with Alex and had a nap. Several hours later a knock came at the door. Unwinding myself from Alex I went to open the door.

Two of my old pack members were there and they had boxes. Allowing them in they went to work putting boxes all over the house. I opened one of the boxes and to my surprise it was Alex's toys.

Smiling I realized while we slept Jaxson had taken over everything. When they were done my parents walked in and begun setting up the house.

 I must have been in shock or something because I just shrugged and went back to lie down with Alex. An hour later when he woke up we went to the lounge room and everything was set up. Cartoons were on the TV and dinner was in the oven.

I left Alex to his own devices and went to check what was for dinner and to my amazement it was lasagna, my favorite. Standing at the door frame I just quietly watched as Alex moved around the lounge room and played with his toys while watching TV.

It was truly amazing that only twenty fours ago our lives were pretty much just like this. Shaking my head I went to dish out dinner and then waited for it to cool.

Having dinner that night was nice and quiet and before I knew it we were both bathed and back in bed in no time at all. Half way through the night I heard a weird noise so waking up quickly I looked around but there was nothing.

Suddenly Alex woke up and projectile vomited all over the bed and himself. Bouncing out of bed with Alex in my arms I rushed him to the bathroom where I undressed him while he was still being sick. Afterward I jumped in the shower with him and just sat there with him in my arms.

After a while the water started cooling so we got out and I got us both dressed. Once done I got a new dummy and put him in the other room while I cleaned everything up. It was dawn before I finally finished everything. Taking out the mattress I was surprised to see Melissa doing the same thing.

"Rough night?"

"Yes I've never seen him sick."

"Human children get sick all the time."

"Not shifter children."

"Oh so…"

"Yeah this isn't normal."

"What do we do?"

"I'm going to ring the pack doctor but I'm just going to wait until Alex wakes up and then try breakfast."

"I think I might do the same thing."

"Good luck."

"And to you too."

I sat down and watched Netflix until Alex got up. When he did I made his normal breakfast of up and go, peanut butter toast and several fruits. The poor little man was that hungry he ate the whole lot and asked for seconds which I agreed.

All morning everything was normal he even ate at lunchtime. I checked in on Melissa and her toddler was completely fine as well. We spent the rest of the day just hanging around and did nothing however once dinner was done and we went to bed it was anything but normal.

Alex again vomited everywhere. This time I rang the pack doctor as I didn't know what to do. Shifters just didn't get sick. Once Alex had settled I got on the phone to the doctor and there was a knock at the door. Walking towards it I was surprised to see Melissa with her toddler in her arms.

I told her to put her toddler with my own while I waited for the doctor to answer.

"DO YOU KNOW WHAT TIME IT IS?"

"I, I know I'm sorry but Alex is sick."

"What do you mean sick?"

"I mean his throwing up this is the second day."

"That's impossible."

"Well it's not, Melissa's toddler is in the same way."

"This is very strange I'll be right over."

"Thank you."

"Don't thank me yet."

Hanging up the phone I went to see what Melissa was doing and she was reading a book to the toddlers. Looking up she smiled at me however I could see it in her eyes she was just as worried as I was.

Nodding my head at her I allowed her to keep reading and waited for the doctor to get here. Within five minutes there was a knock at the door, sighing in relief I went to answer it. To my surprise the doctor was there so was the alpha.

"What are you doing here?"

"The doctor told me what's happening I had to come."

"That's fair enough well come in, they're all in the master bedroom."

Nodding their heads they entered the house and went down the hallway. Once there the doctor did a full check on the children however he deemed them fit and healthy. Both Melissa and I went off like raving lunatics. In the end Jaxson had to yell us down.

"Look the boys seem fine for now all we can do is let them rest."

Both Melissa and I crossed our arms but reluctantly agreed. We promised the doc that if it happened again we would notify him as soon as possible. That ended up being exactly what we did. Melissa and I spent the whole next day with the boys together and that night we watching and waited.

Sure enough a few hours after falling asleep both the boys started vomiting. We grabbed both the boys and threw them in the shower fully clothed and I rang the doctor. He could hear the boys crying and throwing up so hung up straight away and headed over. Melissa and I undressed the boys and made them nice and fresh. When we were sure it was all over we got them out and got them dressed. I heard the front door fly open and went to greet the doctor.

He just shoved straight past me and when straight to the boys. Again he gave them a full body work out and came to the same conclusion.

"I honestly don't know what to tell you ladies."

"Is there nothing you can do?"

"I, I don't know it's so strange."

"I might have an idea."

Turning around Jaxson was standing in my hallway.

"Well?"

"The boys may need to hunt."

"What? They are only two."

"Trust me."

Not knowing what else to do, we all agreed to go hunting the following night. That night both Melissa and I didn't sleep as well as we usually did.

Yes it was in our nature to hunt however they were just toddlers. Devising a few plans we mapped everything out and came up with several plans on how this was going to work.

By dawn we were exhausted but at least we were going to be ready.

During the day my parents and Simon watched the boys so we could nap before nightfall. When the afternoon came around we were woken up to get ready for what was to come.

Worst case scenario the boys just ended up sick again which meant I'd have to personally hunt down that greater alpha. Who better to fix a greater alpha than a greater alpha? All of us stripped naked and set off with the toddlers in tow, it was time to hunt.

Chapter Five

Lachlan

It took several days however before I finally managed to get home. The first few days there I didn't sleep as I set up meetings both with my council members and also tried the supreme council. I had no idea if the supreme council would help me. Wolves had been governing themselves for so long that there were many uncertainties.

Finally managing to lay down I closed my eyes however my mind was racing.

I actually had a mate. What was she doing? Were the children okay? Was the greater alpha evolving and supporting the other toddler he bit?

Were they feeding him right? On and on my brain went until there was a knock at the door. Groaning I got out of bed to answer it. Opening the door I wasn't surprised to see another member there.

"We need to talk."

"Can't it wait until tomorrow?"

"No it can't."

"Come on in."

Walking into my house he made his way to the lounge room and sat down. Taking a seat we just sat there meanwhile our wolves conversed.

"So it is true."

"You will need to be more specific."

"Not only did you allow the greater alpha to stay with his mother but she is also your mate."

"Yeah it's true."

"Well we're here to warn you the others do not approve."

"I kind of gathered that."

"It's more than that, Elijah is rallying everyone to his side."

My head just slumped down. I may now be the oldest on the council however Elijah was hell bent on the old ways. He ruled his region with an iron fist. If no one listened to what he had to say they were either replaced or sadly went missing. This left quite a few packs without alpha's until Elijah found one who would obey him.

"I can deal with Elijah."

"How? He already has three on his side he just needs the other two and me."

"Would you side with him?"

"How can you say that?"

It was true that Damien here had been having a secret affair with a female from another brothers region. I tracked his movements over the years and caught him in the act. He swore blind she was just something to pass the time however he kept going back. Everyone on the council was forbidden to mate as it could cause more greater alphas to be born, it was a 50/50 chance. In the past when it was done the child and mate were instantly killed.

In my time of ruling no one I knew had a child for which I was grateful. I knew it my heart I just couldn't do it.

"Do you love her?"

"She is my mate but I haven't fully claimed her I know what it could cost."

I nodded at my companion. Over the years I, Damien and Richard had relaxed in our ways of governing our regions. Mostly we only stepped in if there were dire circumstances. These were new times and within that people needed to be able to grow and evolve. We still stuck to the old ways but we we're just more relaxed about it.

"So what are we going to do?"

"Well we can't kill him."

"Indeed."

That was our number one rule no killing another council member. If one did step out of line they were taken to the supreme council. That council would then decide what was to happen to that wolf, however again no one in my time broke that law and I didn't intend to do that now.

"Come on man."

"We'll just have to wait and see what happens tomorrow."

"Are you going to fight?"

"My wolf will not allow me not to."

"Oh he's got it bad."

"Indeed what is worse I don't even know the female and we didn't leave on good terms."

"Well you know you'll have my backing."

"I'll always have your back but who else?"
We sat in silence for a while before Damien decided
to up and leave, leaving me alone with my thoughts.
There were normally nine of us however with my
brothers passing there is only I and seven others
now, hopefully making this meeting easier. I only
needed the other three to come to my side. But how
was I going to convince them. Going back to bed I
fell into a restless sleep. The next day I woke half
an hour before the meeting was to start.
As quickly as I could I got up showered, dressed
and eating breakfast running out the door I ended up
coming face to face with none other than Elijah.
"What are you doing here?"
"Fine day for a meeting isn't."
"If you have come to change my mind."
"No in fact I came to warn you. Do what you were
born to do or there will be consequences."
With that he left leaving my wolf reeling. If that
wasn't a threat I didn't know what was. Moving as
quickly as I could I made it to the chambers.
Walking in I was surprised to see that everyone was
there except Damien. Taking my seat at the table I
quietly waited for the proceedings to start.
When Damien finally walked in he looked rather
scared and disheveled. I pulled out a chair for him
however he went to seat between two other alphas.
Although it was a risky business trying to open up a
connection around the other alphas I tried to
connect with Damien however all there was, was

silence. Whatever was going on had him running scared.

"Right, now we're all here let's begin."

"It has come to the council's attention that not only was an alpha unsuccessful at retrieving another alpha   but this alpha has also gotten himself a mate. Now I don't know about all of you but not one but two laws have been broken here today and something needs to be done about it."

My wolf was vibrating rage and it was felt by the surrounding alphas. Some shuddered while others sneer. Getting up I said my peace.

"No laws have been broken."

"How can you say that?"

"For one I have not acted on the mating claim and two the child is secure until a solution can be found."

"If what you say is true it still doesn't hide the fact that you didn't acquire the child which by law we are meant to."

"The child is my mate's I cannot physically acquire the child without harming her."

"Well in that case one of us will go get the child."

"NONE OF YOU WILL GO NEAR HIM."

This time growling resonated around the room. I knew Elijah was going to come at me but this was becoming volatile.

"If you will not acquire the child we will! It is his birth right to be trained and by our side."

"Not at the cost of the female."

"In the past…"

72

"Exactly, in the past, times have changed, people have evolved."

"We obey our laws, it's what's been done for centuries."

"And look what has happened we are cut off from other shifters, we're left to defend for ourselves if there is war. Things have changed."

"Changed for you maybe but not for the rest of us."

"Who here cannot say they haven't wanted a mate? Someone to go home to? Someone to lean on? Someone to just be there when times are tough?"

"We have each other that is our way."

"Our way is over rated."

"The time for talking is over. Show of hands as to who agrees we acquire the child."

Four sets of hands went up. This left myself Damien and another two alphas. The other two just looked at each but said nothing. I looked at my long-time companion but he just stared at the table. I pleaded with him with my eyes to look at me however he just shuddered.

"The law is the law however why not trial the child at home. See if the mother and pack can raise him."

I sighed finally one of the members was seeing sense.

"No! Packs have tried in the past and wars have broken out, packs have been lost."

"That was a long time ago, Damien help me out here."

My friend lifted his head first looking at me and then at Elijah. He went ghostly white and looked

like he was going to puke. Without missing a beat
the other quiet alpha stepped up.

"Let him raise the child with the mother. If nothing
happens before his eighteen birthday then he can
mate the female and we'll deal with the issue then."
Elijah turned bright red however he said nothing. I
looked towards both the other alphas and Damien
however they remained quiet.

"Its four and three maybes if there aren't any
objections we will head out and seek the child
tomorrow."

"Over my dead body."

As everyone left the room a whispered thought went
through my mind.

"That can be arranged."

I waited for everyone to disappear before I went
after Damien not surprisingly I found him at home.
However his home had been ransacked and he was
throwing a million things into a bag.

"What was that back there?"

He looked up at me but it looked like he didn't see
me. He just looked back down and went back to
packing. Since we were away from the other alphas
I opened a connection to Damien and what I found
sent me in a tail spin. His wolf was cowering
whimpering softly while Damien was running
around like a mad man.

"STOP DAMN IT."

He shuttered and dropped to the fall in the fetal
position.

"What is going on let me help you."

All he did was shake his head and start rocking. I got my wolf to reach out to his and what I found was shocking. Elijah had known for years about Damien's mate and threatened to hurt her if he didn't stand down.

I completely lost the plot I grabbed my friend and pulled him to his feet.

"Go to her you have no time for this."

My friend looked at me with fear and gratitude.

"Get your mate, go into hiding and then when the time comes come find me. I'll be at Redwater."

He nodded his head and shot off. Leaving me in the mess I allowed my wolf to rage on in my head.

"We must end him he cannot get our mate."

"We cannot kill another greater alpha it's the law."

"He will get our mate."

"Over our dead body. I'll call the supreme council of greater alphas to Redwater."

"And then what."

"We'll get justice for Damien and also our mate."

"We must leave then."

"Indeed."

I went home and grabbed my travel bag with some clothes and set off. I masked my scent for a few days however on the third day I knew I was being followed. I trekked through several territories before I had, had enough. Making a stand I set up camp and waited them out. It was three days later that they finally attacked.

Relying on my alpha commands I tried to hold them off however some force was driving these wolves to attack. I let my wolf out to his full might and set him loose. We were winning for a while but more and more wolves were upon us.

Every time we attacked they just came back tenfold. After what felt like an eternity things finally started letting up but I was completely exhausted. When the last wolf limped off with a broken leg I collapsed to the ground.

Staying there for several minutes I tried to allow my shifter healing to do its thing however my wolf was going crazy in my mind. He was worried about the pup and his mate. With all my might I stood up and started walking. My wolf was right there was no guarantee these wolves wouldn't go after my mate next.

I walked and ran as fast as I could until I was on the outskirts of Redwater where my body had finally had enough and collapsed. Knowing our mate was close my wolf put all his power into one final howl and closed our eyes. In the dark I didn't ache which was a relief however my mind was trying to wake. It took several moments however finally fighting the fog I managed to remember where I was and why I was there.

I opened my eyes to not only discover I had shifted back to human however I was now surrounded by more unknown wolves. I tried to stand to my full height however my body was too whipped out. Looking around I waited for an attack but none came. Suddenly like a breath of fresh air I hear the most amazing sound I could have ever heard. My mate she was here and she was pissed.

"LET ME THROUGH."

Several wolves allowed her to pass but some stood between us. My wolf growled and a gargling sound resonated from my throat. Several wolves moved in to protect her however this just caused her more distress.

"Let me through you stupid mongrels."

Some moved however they all just watched and waited.

"It took you long enough where have you been."

"It's a long story are you alright and Alex?"

"We're both fine but you have some serious explaining to do let's go."

I tried to get off the ground however my legs just couldn't hold my weight; I just ended up collapsing again. She looked at me for a moment and I could have sworn there was worry there however the look was gone quickly.

"Right several of you change back and carry him to my car. I have clothes food and water. Let's go… NOW!"

The wolves scampered around like she was there alpha. A few changed back to help me to the car and the others ran throughout the forest. When we finally got to the car I was helped in and then we set off. Being just us I explained the situation to her in full detail. Looking at her I could see worry but I could also see rage.

"So this Elijah is coming here now."

"I'm surprised he hasn't already."

"No all has been quiet except for a few things however Melissa, Jaxson and I have been managing just fine without you."

"I can see that but in saying that who were the wolves they're not your old pack."

"Jaxson reached out to any pack that had family members related to ours and surprisingly quite a few alphas have turned up."

"I've only been gone a few days."

"Actually you have been gone for a week and a half and in saying that we have been trying to reach you but no one could get a hold of you."

"After the attack I left my phone and just got here."

"You were attacked."

"Yes a few days ago it seems."

"Do you know by whom? Will they come here? What shit have you gotten us into. By the end of her rant she was rather red and honestly if looks could kill well…"

"I don't know however I couldn't command them. A greater alpha can command any wolf, however these wolves were controlled by another my guess Elijah. I'm guessing he thought he could get me out of the way and the come for you guys."

"Great so we have an army after us and all we have is plain wolves and you."

"It doesn't look good does it?"

"You think… Oh and pray tell why my child is suddenly vomiting over food however raw meat seems totally fine."

"AH yes well I forgot to mention that before I left."

"Mention what exactly."

"Greater alphas are more prone to their animal side, there for they need raw meat to maintain their strength."

"Well that information would have been lovely several days ago thanks."

"I am sorry."

"Not as sorry as you're going to be when this mess is all over."

"I look forward to it."

Closing my eyes I allowed the car to rock me to sleep. Here and smelling my mate I knew it was all going to be okay.

Chapter Six

Amanda

On the drive to the pack I watched the alpha sleep, Casey was quite happy with these events as she felt safe. I however was very conflicted.

I could see he was tired and worn out and I did feel for him, however did I really want another mate? I mean taking on his life span would be amazing but at what cost.

He seemed genuine enough and it did seem he wanted to help us but could I do it all again knowing the cost if something happened to him.

Many thoughts were running through my mind and by the time I got to the pack I still had no answers. Getting out of the car I went to find Alex and to no surprise he was playing with his beta. Picking Alex up I gave him a great big hug.

I knew deep down none of this was his or that alphas fault it was just life but dam I needed a break. Putting Alex back down I watched as he and his beta toddled off. Walking over to Melissa I embraced her in a big hug.

"It's worse than we thought isn't it."

"Indeed I think bourbon is in order."

Melissa nodded her head and went inside. Coming back out she had a bottle and two glasses. Both of us sitting down on her porch I told her everything that the alpha had told me.

By the end of it she had tears in her eyes and a concerned look on her face as she conversed with her wolf. We sat quietly for a moment until we heard the car door open. Looking over I see the alpha walk towards us and he seemed a lot better.

"Have a good sleep."

"The best I've had for a while."

We all stood quietly for a moment before Melissa spoke to the alpha.

"So what is your name?"

My jaw dropped to the floor this was meant to be my mate and I didn't even know his name. Cheeks reddened I waited for an answer.

"My names Lachlan I should of told use that but with everything going on."

Melissa whispered in my ear however with shifter hearing Lachlan would have heard it easily enough.

"His quite cute."

Completely embarrassed my cheeks darkened still further.

"You know he can hear you right?"

"Oh my god I'm so sorry I forgot."

"It's alright when we join a pack we can mind speak all we want."

"I can speak to Simon."

"Yes mates don't need a pack to speak to each other. That magic comes from your bond."

"She is right but how don't you all have a pack."

"Jaxson is having a little trouble with Alex's wolf."

"Maybe I can help."

"Highly doubtful but go nuts."

Lachlan walked over to where the boys were playing and sat on the group. They all actually sat there for some time. Melissa and I just looked at each other dumbfounded. None of us could get the boys to sit for more than two seconds.

Even our routines were out of whack because the boys kept sorting each other out. Eventually they all walked over and the little ones had big smiles on their faces. Melissa and I looked at each other this was going to be trouble.

"Mommy."

"Can you…"

"Can I what sweetie?"

He looked towards Lachlan however he just nodded his head.

"Mummy and mummy friend on floor."

Melissa and I nodded our heads. Melissa actually sat on her butt which had me giggling.

"No on your knee's Hun."

"Oh okay I didn't know."

"We'll get you there don't worry." Alex continued.

"I."

"I."

"Names."

"Melissa."

"Amanda."

"Here by join the pack of the greater alpha. I will obey our heritage and laws from this day forth."

Both Melissa and I said everything Alex said and both giggled. This was serious business however it was just funny coming from one so small."

"Mommy."

Holy hell Alex was inside my mind. Melissa looked just as shocked as I was but she was looking at her toddler.

"I'm guessing use can hear the boys."

Both of us still stunned just nodded our heads. Lachlan had actually done it, we were a pack. Getting off the ground I embraced Alex in a great big hug and kissed him all over. Between the diet and now this we were finally getting places.

Asking Melissa to watch the toddlers I ran to my parent's house and chased down Simon. Within half an hour everyone was connected.

It would have been a great thing however the boys had no way of shutting off the connection to the pack so everyone was getting a play by play. Some of the things they were saying were idle toddler chit chat however they were planning a little escape. Everyone watched and waited.

Sure enough they tried creeping away. Melissa and I quickly gave chase however that's when playful and fun turned sour.

"Let us go."

Lachlan and Simon came rushing over to catch us before we fell. No choice but to let the toddlers go, we look at Lachlan for help.

"This is why we don't have packs. Toddlers are unpredictable with their power."

"What are we going to do?"

"In time they will learn right from wrong for now I will guide and help when I can. You ladies go sit down I'll follow and guide them."

I wasn't sure but I looked at the others and they were all nodding their heads.

"Alright just keep them safe."

They didn't come back for several hours. Melissa and I were starting to panic when a rustling came from the bushes beside the house. Out came Lachlan and two very bloodied up pups. Melissa and I groaned. It was going to take forever to get the blood off.

"Well at least I don't have to hunt tonight come on you pair."

The little pups ran inside and then the chase was on. They knew it was bath time however they refused to. Melissa and I ended up playing a game of cat and mouse with the pups until Lachlan put his foot down and they stopped in their tracks. Scooping up the pups we took them to the shower and did the long process of getting them clean.

When we were finally done they popped back into their human forms and got dressed. Once done we put them to bed and then closed the door. Sighing in relief we made our way to the lounge room where everyone was silently waiting. Lachlan walked over and handed us a glass which we gratefully took and downed in one go. Melissa spluttered a little but all in all said thanks and went to sit with Simon.

"You can all go home the boys can sleep together here tonight."

"Are you sure what if something happens?"

"Will be okay Lachlan will be here."

"I will be?"

"Yes but in the spare room."

A look of disappointment crossed his face but it was gone quick enough. Casey whimpered in my mind however I just ignored her. One by one everyone hugged us and left. In the end it was just Lachlan and I. Sitting on the lounge I just leaned back and closed my eyes. Today was a trying day and we had many more to come.

"Are you alright?"

"Does it look like I am?"

"I'm sorry this happened to you."

"Yeah me too."

Lachlan went to my kitchen where he poured us both a drink and came out with a new bottle.

"Here I think we both are going to need this."

Gratefully taking the glass I downed it in one go and poured another.

"Is it always going to be like this?"

"Unfortunately yes. To be a greater alpha you need to be raised by one."

Sighing I downed this drink too. It would take a while but a shifter could get drunk after two or three bottles. I just needed to feel the burn at the back of my throat.

"So what do we do now?"

"Unfortunately all we can do is wait."

"Seems like all we do these days. Packs are flying in from everywhere."

"That is a good thing more protection for the pups."
"You mean toddlers."
"Yes sorry. I haven't had to raise one but I've heard the stories."
"Does it get any easier?"
"Depends on the child and these are different circumstances again."
"Maybe I should have let you take him."
"Don't say that."
"Maybe, maybe not, but it is so friggen hard."
"It will all work out in the end I assure you."
"I sure hope so."
We just sat and drank in silence, just after midnight I called it quits and went to bed. I was a little buzzed but I knew that would wear off quick. Jumping into bed I slipped down to my bra and panties and snuggled in. Sighing I drifted off in a restless sleep. It must have been the early hours of the morning but I heard an ear splitting scream. Jumping up as fast as I could I go to the boys.

Both were in wolf form and were resonating power. Lachlan came flying up behind me saw the situation and transformed. He was the most beautiful gigantic black wolf I had ever seen.

He walked into the room and lay down on the floor. The pups in no time at all circled

up in-between his paws and went back to sleep. Thanking Lachlan I leaned on the door frame as finally he went to sleep too.
I never thought about having any more children after Alex but the images in my mind had my ovaries vibrating.
Smiling at the little group I left them and went back to bed. It wasn't until several hours later that morning when I woke up and the most amazing smell hit my nostrils.
 Putting on a robe I went to investigate. Both the boys back in toddler form were sitting on the kitchen counter watching Lachlan cook. He had mountains of food already laid out and by the looks of it was just finishing pancakes.
I was just as transfixed as the boys however I was watching Lachlan's movements and not his cooking skills. My belly fluttered and my pussy clenched. It had been a long time since I was turned on and he left nothing to the imagination. Well-toned back and his arse in those boxers damn.
A growl came out of his mouth and I was highly embarrassed as he must have been smelling my arousal. I quickly went to the safety of the dining room and waited for the boys to join me.
A few slow deep breaths later I managed to get myself under control however when they all walked in my eyes went to Lachlan's

crotch. Those boxer shorts left me drooling. He wasn't wearing any underwear and by dam that looked like a mouthful.

I quickly averted my eyes however he saw my look and a big smile came over his face. Quickly getting up I place both the boys in a sit and dished out their breakfast. The food was absolutely amazing. Even the toddlers where digging in. By the time everyone was full the toddlers went to the lounge room to play and I went to get dressed. Coming out of my room I ran into Lachlan who was coming out of the bathroom and be damn I couldn't help the growl.

Excusing myself I went to check the boys and luckily enough they were just sitting down playing cars together. Sitting down quietly I just watched the boys play until Melissa came over to get her son.

Afterward I sat Alex at the table to do some learning. Since having to move to the pack his education had been put on me and boy was it trying.

Everything had to be done in the right order or all hell broke loose.

As we began a mathematical puzzle Lachlan joined us and just watched. Alex did it in no time at all and Lachlan looked proud. It wasn't until I tried to get Alex to do random numbers that Lachlan got to see the extent of how challenging Alex was. I picked up a ten instead of the four and his eyes glowed. My neck went straight up in submission and Lachlan slammed his hands on the table.

"You might be only two years old little man but you DON'T EVER make your mother submit like that. Do you understand?"

Alex lowered his head and said sorry.

"Is he like this all the time?"

"Yes but we're slowly getting better. Today seems like a bad day."

"Maybe allow him to go to the packs play group."

"I couldn't. I mean if he's like this with me how would he be with them?"

"That is true, how about I take the boys and see how we go."

"I don't know what if something happens?"

"Come with us then."

"I don't know."

"What's the worst thing that can happen?"

Giving in Lachlan and I took Alex with the permission of Jaxson to the packs play group. He tried to get the teacher and the kids to submit to him however Lachlan put him straight in his place.

Though I couldn't hear the conversation there was a few times when Alex went up to the teacher and the kids and apologized.

By the end of the day we all agreed that Alex could attend however Lachlan had to be there but he was more than happy to.

Not wanting to hunt again tonight but needing to take the toddlers. I undressed and got Alex to do the same. I turned to ask Lachlan if he wanted to join us however he was already undressed and just staring at me.

Looking at him I saw his dick go half masked and quickly turned away to transform.

"Mummy can we go now?"

"Sure thing sweetie let's go."

I went at a slower pace for Alex but Lachlan's wolf went brawling past. All I could think of was bloody males. They really had no control over there wolves when a female was about.

Sure enough by the time we tracked him down he had killed a buck and was wagging his tail eagerly.

"Mummy he awesome."

"Bloody show off, I could have done the same."

"But he's our mate it's what they do."

"Now is not the time Casey its Alex's dinner time."

Letting out a warning growl I watched as Lachlan backed off. Ripping open the buck I went and laid down and watched Alex dig in. It was a bloody free for all. After a while I nodded to Lachlan who bounced over and dug in. Casey was so happy and content with this interaction she kept quiet but happily wagged our tail. My eyes eventually started to close however I heard a growl. Looking over both Lachlan and Alex were fighting over a huge chunk of meat.

"Alex let it go."

"No mummy mine."

Not knowing what else to do I went and grabbed Alex by his butt and tried to pull him away. This just caused more growling from both the alphas. I looked up to get help from Lachlan but the twit was happily wagging his tail.

Clearly getting enjoyment out of the situation I let go of Alex and huffed. Seemingly neither alpha wanted to give up the big chunk of meat, I went and lay down. After a while Alex came over to me and surprisingly he had the huge chunk of meat.

"You're not going to eat all that."

"Yes I am it is mine."

"You're going to get a tummy ache."

He just growled and toddled off with the big chunk of meat in-between his legs. Looking at Lachlan I growled at him for being irresponsible however he just gave me a lopsided grin and then kept eating. Bloody males!

Chapter Seven

Lachlan

Spending time with Alex and his mum
Amanda was a whirlwind of happy times
and also frustrating times. Having a mini
alpha around was defiantly time consuming.
The two things I did learn was the little
alpha was in fact very smart for his age and
also his mother was an amazing woman.
Having to raise Alex on her own and
fighting death to keep him, no wonder she
was conflicted about the mating.

Once knowing her history my wolf and I
backed off but we could see her looking at
us from time to time. This made my wolf
very happy but also sad.

He could see the wonder in her eyes but the
grief was rolling off her in spades.

Everything around the territory seemed
completely normal however I knew Elijah
was just bidding his time. It would have
gotten back to him that I hadn't died.

Leaving Amanda and Alex alone for the day
I decided to check in on the alpha Jaxson. I
knew it wouldn't be easy being around so
many alphas let alone two greater ones.

Knocking at his door I waited for an answer.
"Come in."

93

Walking in I see several others there and none looked too please to see me.

"Has there been any sightings?"

"One or two but they quickly left before we could capture them"

"Elijah will make his move soon then."

"We'll be watching alpha go home to your mate."

"She isn't my mate yet."

"She will come around."

"I hope so."

Leaving the alphas I actually did go in search and to my surprise she had the boys training. In a massive play pen in the front yard were the two toddlers and they were trying to catch rabbits.

Trying being the key word as they were bouncing on them and then letting them go. Laughing and shaking my head I walked up and sat next to Amanda.

"So how is it going?"

"Terrific as you can see."

I could see. One of the pups had a rabbit by its tail and was pulling it around the yard.

"This seems cruel to me."

"I know but they have to learn. You cannot be there for their first kill."

"I know but for now can't they just be boys. You know playing with toys, watching TV…"

"Hunting rabbits."

"I know, I know it's funny because sometimes I wish things were different but times like this I feel like it is normal you know. Shifters doing what shifters do."

"I know what you mean love."

As soon as I said that she went ridged before I could apologized she turned and smile at me. Relaxing we just continued watching the boys until Melissa and Simon came over.

"So they're not dead yet?"

"Nope I think it's just a game now."

Amanda said and smiled at Melissa.

These two had become the best of friends since Melissa changed and it was good to see. Amanda wasn't alone in all of this. Sure I was here but I was just for guidance at least for now. Just then my phone rang and I excused myself. Looking it was a private number. I was going to leave it but something in me made me answer it.

"Who is this?"

"It's Damien."

"Thank god where are you? Are you safe?"

"I am but I have some bad news."

"Well."

"Two council members are dead."

"WHAT, HOW?"

"I don't know but wolves are traveling."

"ELIJAH."

"I'm coming to you we need protection."

"Come to Redwater I'll alert the alphas here it's time I took this to the supreme alphas."

"How do you know if they will help?"

"I don't but we must try. I refuse to kill another alpha without consent."

"Even if he's killed first."

"I will not stoop to his level. Come brother after you arrived I'll go."

Getting off the phone I look towards little alphas group of family and friends. If the supreme alphas didn't help us I may not have a choice but to kill him. Sighing I left the happy little pack and went back to the alpha.

The news I had to share was none to pleasing but he took it in stride. He said he would get more packs involved and widen the perimeter. On the way back I made another call. This was to a long-time friend to us wolves. I silently sat in the background and watched.

"Marcus hey."

"Lachlan how are you?"

"I need that meeting."

"That bad."

"Two alphas are dead, a friend is on the move and the other is going to make a move on the toddler."

"How do you know all this?"

"The youngest Damien he's on his way, my guess is with his mate as well."

"Shit man, I'm sorry I'll try again to organize something if they come around where do you want to meet?"

"Redwater you know it?"

"No but leave it with me?"

After Marcus hung up I went straight to my mate and the toddlers. There was no way anyone was coming near the kids. I didn't know if the toddlers managed to kill a rabbit or if they finally got help however they were playing tug of war with one.

Both happily growling away at the other. Amanda must have seen something on my face as she told Melissa to watch the kids. Nodding her head we went inside away from the others.

"How bad is it?"

"It's bad."

"What are we going to do we can't stay here forever. The others…"

"They know what they signed up for, we however need to prepare."

"So it's going to happen."

"It is, two members of the council are dead and wolves from all over are on the move. Some may stand with us but if Elijah gets to them first?"

"So we run."

"Running will make it worse think of the boys."

"I, I don't know I can't lose Alex too."

I walked up to her and wrapped my arms around her, to my surprise she held me back. If we had been mated my wolf could have soothed hers but at this point in time there was no pushing the subject. All in all I was happy to hold her and my wolf was going crazy over her smell.

"I've rung a member of the supreme council again I'm hoping he will come through."

She sighed and held me tighter. Jaxson came flying through the front door.

"There is another regional alpha here."

"Are you sure where abuts?"

"Just on the outskirts of town he's surrounded but he has a pregnant female with him."

"Shit that must be Damien he must have been closer than I thought lead the way."

Jaxson went outside and I looked down at my potential mate.

"Go we will be alright."

"If you're sure?"

"Your friend needs you."

I leaned down and placed a kiss on her forehead much to my surprise she closed her eyes and inhaled deeply. Letting her go was hard and my wolf happily protested however he knew of the danger to come so he transformed. It took twenty minutes to get to them and much to my relief it was Damien and his mate. Transforming back I embraced my friend.

"I didn't know you were this close."

"We have been traveling for days, hiding when we smelt others, sleeping in known packs."

"Well it is good to see you my friend come."

We all transformed back and headed off. While on the move Damien told me in great detail the massacre that bestowed the other two alphas and the few wolves that were following Elijah. My wolf howled out loud for the loss of our companions and started plotted Elijah's demise.

When we finally arrived everyone had gone inside so we all transformed back and dressed before I knocked on my mate's door. When she opened it the worry evaporated from her face and a relived smile was in its place.

"Room for two more."

"Yes of course come in, come in make yourselves at home."

Everyone walked in and sat in the lounge room. Damien's mate introduced herself to mine and then went gooey over her toddler. They went off to the toddler's room with smiles while Damien and I sat sombre in the lounge room. Neither of us knew what to say.

Eventually I went and got us two glasses and poured us a drink. Handing one to Damien I sat back down.

"To those we have lost. May you rest in peace and justice be swift."

Lifting our glasses we toasted then drank. Poor Damien was that out of sorts he drank it all in one go.

"Hey we'll get them justice I swear to it."

All he did was just nod his head. I knew exactly how he felt. My mate wasn't pregnant however if she lost her son.

Well there wasn't anything I wasn't capable of I'd get him back. The females eventually joined us, mine sitting next to me with her hand on my knee and Damien's sitting on his lap. We were quietly talking among ourselves when I realized my mate couldn't join in.

"Hey um guys you will need to speak out loud, I um we aren't connected yet."

"So use aren't mated?"

"It's complicated."

"Ah I see it's another man isn't it?"

Damien was just trying to be funny however the hurt on my mates face said it all. My wolf growled causing me to growl in turn making Damien go rather white.

"Hey sorry I was joking."

"I know but it hit quite close to home."

"It's alright it was a few years ago. You see my first mate died then Lachlan came along."
"Oh I'm sorry for your loss."
"As he said it's complicated."
Damien nodded his head however we all fell silent. Alex feeling his mother's distress came running in and sat on her lap.
"Mummy you okay?"
"I'm okay darling."
She swept some hair out of his eyes and kissed his forehead. Alex turned his attention to the new comers.
"NO."
I had to hold my mate as Alex suddenly jumped out of her arms and went towards Damien. Both of their eyes glowing while the females cowered, the power was too much for them to handle. I stood up and yelled at them both. Damien stopped doing whatever he was doing and Alex went sobbing to his mum.
"What the hell do you think you're doing?"
"I was testing his wolf."
"Are you stupid? You caused the females distress!"
He looked towards his mate and apologized profusely. Both females were shaking and trying to get their breath back.
"Never do that again."

"I, I I'm sorry baby are you okay and the baby."

"We're fine but he shore is one powerful greater alpha, no wonder Elijah wants all of us."

"What do you mean us?"

"He's coming after me in the hopes the baby will be a greater alpha too."

"But there's no guarantee?"

"He doesn't care he's coming regardless." This situation was getting out of hand and our only hope now was to keep everyone safe until the supreme council arrived. Everyone sat quietly for a while not knowing what to say.Over the next few weeks wolves came and went from the territory but no one attacked. In the end the alpha Jaxson started sending everyone home. The rest of us on my word knew we weren't safe. I watched, I observed and I waited. All the women would go hunting with Damien or I so they weren't alone but everyone was feeling the stress. The only good thing was the little alpha and his beta were none the wiser.

They practiced hunting with rabbits and due to their power were maturing at a great rate. Sure there was incidents where I had to step in however all in all it seemed the pack was dealing with it all rather well. In my times alone I thought of my brothers, both the ones that were murdered and the ones backing Elijah. In these times I would creep away getting several miles from the pack so I could release my pent up grief and rage. Returning to the pack was never easy at these times the little alpha felt what I was feeling and would either wake and seek out his mother or sleep in my arms in pup form. It had me dreaming of non-stressful times, lying in my mates arms or raising several pups of our own.

Amanda though she wouldn't admit it was slowly coming around. She would rub my head in wolf form or allow me to train her son alone. Our mating was a slow process for now.

Finally after a month of waiting my phone rang it was the supreme council they agreed the situation had gotten out of hand and were willing to come speak with us all.

More protection from Elijah was a bonus. It was arranged for the next clouded night as a few had to fly in.

When I told everyone the news they began to relax. Thinking this was almost over even I was relaxed and just hung out with everyone however deep down I was afraid my time here was almost up.

Keeping an eye on the weather reports we saw there was cloud cover and possible rain

due in the coming days. Everyone was
vibrating with excitement.

Even the toddlers became erratic due to our
moods. The last day before the meeting we
all took the boys out hunting one last time.
None of us knew what was to come but we
all knew our time here was over. Everyone
in wolf form surrounded the pups while all
the females tracked and hunted.

When the females pulled down a couple of
bucks everyone settled in for the night.
Looking at my future mate I nodded my
head and took off to scout the area.

I wasn't even gone ten minutes when a
warning howl ripped through the air. Racing
back towards the pack my way ended up
being block by no other than Elijah and the
two other greater alphas.

"So brother is has come to this."

"By the time were done with you the female
and pups will be long gone."

"Over my dead body."

"That's what the others said as well."

"So you admit it you killed them."

"You left me no choice."

"There is always a choice."

The time for talking was over as a group
they pounced on me. I may have been the
oldest greater alpha left but our powers and
strength were the same. It was a bloody
battle. All fur, tooth and claw. After a while

several other wolves joined the fray for which I was grateful. It was Jaxson his beta and Damien. Damien took on one alpha while Jaxson and his beta took the other. This left me with Elijah.

Though my energy was fading I had to end this. Running full force into Elijah I tried to grab at his neck to snap it however he slammed me to the side. As I was getting up there was no time for defense he grabbed my leg snapping it instantly.

Howling out I tried to shrug him off but he managed to grab another leg snapping it too. Rolling me over he was going to gouge out my stomach but a wolf came flying out of nowhere and managed to shift him to the side.

Looking at the wolf it was no other than my mate and she was pissed. Eyes glowing golden she summoned the whole pack to her side. Having no choice but to watch I waited to see what would happen next, to my surprise Elijah looked like he smiled and took off.

I tried to get up and assess the situation however my legs broke again. Howling in pain I just lay on the ground. Feeling completely hopeless I had to wait for someone to come to me.

"Brother."

"Is everyone alright?"

"My mate she's…"
A howl so full of grief and loss ripped
through the forest. That meant only one
thing not only was Damien's mate gone but
so were the boys. This was entirely my fault.

Chapter Eight

Amanda

The pain was completely ripping me apart. I didn't know what to do. My baby was gone. The babies were gone and so was Damien's mate. Melissa came and sat by me and howled along with me.

I thought the grief of losing a mate was bad but this, this I was going to losing my friggen mind over, Casey along with me. Everyone in the pack came over and surrounded us. No one said anything, everyone just sat with us in our moment of grief.

Eventually Jaxson and Damien came over in human form. Hoping for answers or a plan I begged Casey to return us to human form which she complied.

"So what do we do now?"

Damien hung his head at a loss so I looked at Jaxson.

"I, I, I don't know, I'm so sorry Amanda."

"Don't be, we will get them back."

Everyone looked at me like I was crazy but a breath of fresh air spoke up.

"She's right we will get them back the council will be here tomorrow."

"What are they going to do?"

"Hopefully track down those arseholes and rip them to shreds."

"AMANDA."

"Jaxson you can't deny your thinking the same thing."

"I, yes well…"

"Well nothing. THEY TOOK OUR BABIES. He took your best friends child."

"I, I know, let's see what tomorrow holds."

I transformed into my she-wolf and took off for home.

Hoping to be left alone I made it in no time at all. Stepping inside I could smell my baby he was everywhere. Casey let out a whimper.

"I know Hun we'll get him back I promise."

Ignoring me she smelt and whimpered all through the house. Coming to Alex's room she nudged it opened. Seeing through her eyes I could see what she was, feeling, loss and emptiness.

She went and jumped on Alex's bed and curled up into a ball. Tears streaming down onto her fur: We stay quietly together in the dark with nothing but our memories to haunt us. The whole time I thought what would Alexander have done?

After a long while a slight tap came at the door, it was Lachlan. Casey yipped at him and he went straight to us. I may have been conflicted about him but I was glad he was here.

"I'm so sorry guys I should have stayed with you."

Casey lifted her head and put it on his lap, she and I were on the same page this wasn't his fault. We all got lax and in the end ambushed, there seriously was nothing no one could of done except die. Lachlan put his hand on our head and scratched behind our ears.

Before I knew it we went to sleep.

Waking up the next day I was very much naked, sometime throughout the night we had transformed back. I lay there quietly contemplating the situation. Yes Lachlan was here however he was still fully clothed and sleeping quietly, or so I hoped.

As quietly and gently as I could I tried to get up. Almost managing to stand Lachlan let out a growl. I completely froze half on half off the bed waiting for him to wake however he didn't bat an eye.

Finally managing to stand I went to walk away but something inside me stopped me in my tracks. I turned my face towards Lachlan and just watched him sleep. At this moment in time my need for a companion grew. Lachlan didn't have to be here, he didn't have to help us but he did. Casey whimpered in my mind and this drew the mating call forth. Could I really give my heart to another mate? Yes I was scared history would repeat itself however wasn't life about taking risks?

Taking a chance with the unknown that was a different story.

Lachlan drew in a deep breath and a smile slowly crept upon my face. Maybe just maybe I would give this male a chance however for now I had to get ready.

Creeping my way out of the room I made my way to my own room.

Quickly getting dressed I proceeded to make my way outside and wait for everyone to show up. Sitting on the step I closed my eyes and breathed in the morning scents. Hearing steps coming towards me I open my eyes to find Melissa walking towards me. I nodded my head and she came flying at me. Managing to open my arms up in time she hit me with an OOF.

"Hey it's alright we'll get them back I promise."

"How can you be so sure?"

"I have faith in Lachlan."

"But the council?"

"We're all in this together. If I have to I will chase those bastards down myself."

"Oh no you mustn't."

"We'll see, for now we wait."

And wait we did. The whole pack came to sit with us as did Lachlan and Jaxson. Around lunchtime Lachlan got a call. Walking away he answered it.

Watching him quietly I could see his body tense up and his fist go into a ball. Letting go of Melissa I walked over to him and placed my hand on his shoulder. For a moment he looked at me and said nothing.

"I agree." He hung up the phone.

"What's the matter?"

"Now is not the time the council is here."

Nodding my head I followed Lachlan back to the others. He told everyone the council was at the border waiting and we had to leave immediately.

Everyone quickly got undressed and followed Lachlan into the woods. It was eerily quiet without the pups with us. I heard a whimper and turn to see Simon lean over and give Melissa a lick on her face. Part of me was jealous but part of me was glad she had a strong mate at her side.

Within an hour we were at the northern edge of Jaxson's pack and several different smells invaded my   nostrils. Letting out a growl Casey stood straight at defense.

 Lachlan turned his head toward us but said nothing. I knew these people were here to help but there was so many different creatures and one I wasn't sure of.

111

Lachlan transformed and got dressed.
Looking to my son's pack I nodded my head
and we all did the same.
"Thank you for coming."
"We shouldn't even be here."
I let out a low growl and the man eyed me
quietly.
"I assure you we mean peace."
"Tell that to the she-wolf."
"You must excuse her elders for it is her
child that was taken."
"Why is this a problem for the council your
people have governed yourselves for many
years."
"That is true elder however I um you see…"
"Argh yes I see which one is it."
"It is me."
They all looked at me shocked.
"The greater alpha you smell around us isn't
her mate but her child and these are his
pack."
"This is getting interesting indeed continue."
"You see my brother died and I came to get
the child to be raised as one of my brother's
however I ran into a snag."
"By snag you mean the child's mother."
"Yes sir. I went back to the wolf council and
pleaded my case however it fell on death's
door, not long after a greater alpha went on
the run and another two were killed."
All the members of the council growled.

"Killing another greater alpha is forbidden."
"It is forbidden in our laws too, however this greater is crafty he's using other wolves and two other greater alphas to do his dirty work. We were ambushed, the children were taken and a mate."
"Who's mate was taken and why?"
"Mine I am one of the greater alphas, my mate is pregnant."
"So the plot thickens. So what would you have us do?"
"Help us. Being the oldest greater alpha I will join your ranks."
"You have got to be kidding."
"No elder please this is my family."
My eyes must have nearly popped out of my head in shock because everyone turned to look at me.
"You haven't even mated her yet?."
"It's complicated."
"What isn't complicated with you wolves?"
The man sighed and turned to around looking at his fellow members.
"We will discuss this but there is no guarantee this is after all a wolf problem."
I see Lachlan bowed his head. Anger literally rippled through my body on the verge of transforming I took a step forward however Lachlan grabbed my arm and shook his head.

"This cannot be it damn it Lachlan we want our families back."

"There is nothing more I can say he is right. Without a wolf on the council we may just have to go it alone."

"NO DAMN IT…"

"Hush do not piss them off they are the oldest of old. Older than me and way more powerful."

"I cannot stand this."

"And you won't have to. Hi I'm Marcus."

A council man came walking towards us. Smelling him automatically made me growl out loud.

"Easy she-wolf I will not harm you."

"What are you?"

"Well let's just say I am on your side."

He followed that sentence up with a wink which in turn made Lachlan growl.

"Easy old friend I know she is yours."

Unable to help myself I scoffed causing the elder to laugh out loud. Lachlan looked down at me and I held my head in shame. I really was coming around however the toddlers were more important at the moment. The elder quietly looked between us and then shook his head.

"We have made a decision."

Everyone turned their heads towards the supreme council members and waited.

"Marcus here will help you get your pups and your mate greater alpha, but we want something in return?"

"Anything please we are wasting time."

"Actually you aren't we have our own trackers out there right now following the rogue greater alpha. Everyone is safe."

I wanted to breathe a sigh of relief however the alpha was looking at me for lack of a better word evilly.

"You two must be mated and Lachlan will be the wolf member for the supreme council."

"Is that it?"

"If only! There will soon be another three dead greater wolf alphas and if Lachlan here joins us the wolves will need a sixth. Lachlan must track down and find the new members."

"But, but… that could take years. Besides I'm not a council member yet another won't come to being until I am."

"These are our terms alpha take it or leave it?"

"Lachlan no we can't."

"SHHH. It will all be alright."

He gently moved a hand down my face. Looking into my eyes I could see his longing but I could also see pain. He knew what I went through the first time I lost a mate. He looked back towards the council.

"How long do we have to decide?"

"48 hours after that you're on your own."
Lachlan bowed his head and then looked back towards me. Looking into his eyes I was totally conflicted. Could I really mate this man only for him to have to walk away? Hearing the members walk away I turned to look at my sons pack.

I could see the pain on my parents faces but it was Melissa's face that crushed me the most. There was hope and it was hope I would do the right thing.

Changing back into my wolf I didn't return to Jaxson's pack I went home. When I got there I transformed and went to my old room and dressed. The house smelt stale and felt cold and empty. This was what I needed. Empty and nothing smelt like my son or our family.

 I went to the linen cupboard and got out a blanket, I then proceed to go and lie on the lounge. Everyone's future yet again relied on me.

What the hell was I going to do? Silently crying I fell into a restless sleep.

Many hours later a soft knock came at the door. Groaning I hid under the blanket and hoped whoever it was would just go away.

"She-wolf I know you're in there."
It was that guy Marcus how had he found me? Groaning again I said to come in then

sat up on the lounge. Marcus walked in and
then looked around.

"Well this is cozy."

"What do you want?"

"Just to talk."

"Why?"

"Because Lachlan is a good guy."

"Don't you think I know that?"

"Then what is the issue?"

"You don't know?" He just sat quietly
staring at me.

"My son his dad…"

"Go on."

"He died."

"I figured that out as I knew the boy wasn't
Lachlan's; however this does not explain
your behavior."

"I should be dead if it wasn't for my son I
would be."

"I know how a mating works."

"Have you ever and I mean ever literally
lived and breathed for one person. To have
one little teeny tiny   glimmer of happiness
in the dark. To just live for that and nothing
else because you know your mate would
have wanted you to go on without them."

"No I don't."

"Exactly and then in comes mister tall,
powerful and handsome and it makes you
rethink life."

"So you do like him?"

117

"I don't know he seems nice, I wanted to kill him at the start."

"Ah yes Lachlan explained his little predicament. I admit I had a good laugh at his expense."

"Well I can't go through it all again okay. I lost one mate if I lost another I, I, I don't know."

"Your problem is your heart and that pup of yours."

"Excuse me?"

"It all comes down to you worrying about your son. It's not the loss of a mate but the loss of your son." This creature was maddening if Lachlan's voice wasn't inside my mind I would be within my right to bite this man and no it wouldn't be sexy. I jumped of the lounge and went to head outside.

"I wouldn't do that if I were you?"

"Oh and why not?"

"Because Lachlan is waiting behind that door."

I stood frozen with my hand on the handle. If I turned it I would have to face the truth and an unknown future. If I stayed inside I could quite possibly piss of a council member. I decided to remove my hand from the door and walk back to the lounge.

"She-wolf…"

"My name is Amanda."

"Okay Amanda I don't know what you're going through however answer me two questions."

"If I do will you go?"

"Yes."

"Fine."

"My first question is you fought through the loss once before why are you so sure you won't be able to do it again? You pair seem like a great she-wolf and mother so why deny yourselves and your child a better future with him?"

I literally felt like this man smacked me clean across the face. It was true I made it through the loss because I had Alex. I lived and breathed for my child however Alex really did like Lachlan and was fond of him. Marcus must have seen the conflict I was going through because he nodded his head and silently left.

I heard murmurs outside however I didn't pay attention. My mind was going through the memories of Lachlan and Alex and there were many.

A lot of it was Lachlan teaching Alex about being a greater alpha, however there was the hunting, the playing, the sleeping, the respect and now thinking about it the love I saw in Lachlan's eyes.

Even though we weren't mated and he wasn't Alex's dad he was stepping into the role of mate and father. For the first time in a very long time I wasn't alone I did in fact have a mate by my side.

He never pushed me and his whole world had become Alex and I.

Why hadn't I seen it sooner? My grief had in fact blinded me to life and the many good things I could have had. But that's when the memories stopped.

Casey whimpered in my mind as a new pain shot through our system. Soon enough we were going to have a new mate however would the loss kill us and if so what about Alex?

Chapter Nine

Lachlan

Thanks to Jaxson Marcus and I tracked down Amanda quick enough however it was Marcus was the one that went inside to her. Even though Marcus wouldn't touch her or wasn't even into her for that matter I couldn't help but be jealous. When he finally came outside I went forwards to go in however he placed a hand on my shoulder to stop me.

"Leave her be for now."

"But she is in pain."

"I know however she needs to figure out all of this on her own."

Nodding my head I went to the tree line and transformed into my wolf. Cade and I stayed like that until the following dawn. We heard the whimpers throughout the night and even our mates howl but we didn't enter. The pain was not only deafening but gut wrenching.

I felt like a terrible person for coming into her life. She and Alex were better off without me. I should have let her renounce my claim then none of this would be happening.

When the door opened she stood there looking around.

"I know you're here Lachlan come inside."

Cade made us yep with excitement. Transforming I got dressed and walked out of the tree line. Surprisingly she had a smile on her face. She turned and walked into the house, me hot on her tail. When I stepped in she had sat down and asked me to do the same.

"Before you say anything I just want to say I am sorry."

"What for?"

"If I hadn't come none of this would be happening."

"That is true however Alex would still be gone."

Damn why did she have to be right.

"So I want to go through with the mating."

Luckily I was seated or I would have fallen over, she continued.

"You have been good to me and to Alex. You have been caring and understanding and if I'm not mistaken loving?"

Was she a witch? How could she have known? Sure the mating was everything with us wolves however the time spent with her and her sons pack... I did fall in love with her.

"How did you know?"

"I wasn't too sure but I am now."

"So what are we going to do?"

"You're going to take me on a date and then make love to me. Afterward and only afterward will I allow you to claim me."

"As the lady wishes."

"One other thing."

"Sure, yes anything."

"Don't disappear on me just yet I couldn't take it."

I practically jumped out of my chair and landed on my knees in front of her. Putting my hands over hers which were resting on her legs I looked up into her eyes. Looking at me I could see tears ready to fall however her eyes sparkled with determination. She was in fact one strong powerful she-wolf and if I hadn't known better I'd have sworn she was an alpha.

Reaching up I gently caressed her face and that was when the first tear fell. It took everything in me to not hold her but I had to do this right.

"I know your fear is me leaving and never returning but that is not the case I swear it."

"How can you be so sure?"

"I don't but I have two things worth fighting for."

I leaned up and placed a gently kiss on her cheek. Standing up I explained that I had to get ready for our date. She nodded her head and wiped at her tears.

"Yes same I'll um see you in town soon."
Nodding my head I left her alone. Cade was
all but ready to jump out of my skin but I
had to remind him not yet. Crossing the
lawn I went to transform however I was
greeted by Marcus.
"So you finally got her."
"No not yet I um have to take her on a date."
Marcus looked at me for a moment and then
pissed himself laughing.
"Wow that is very human of you."
"It's not what I had in mind but this is to
help her."
"Your pussy whipped without the pussy my
friend."
"How did you even get here?"
"Oh I have my ways."
"Right well I have to go."
"Don't do anything I wouldn't do."
Marcus walked off back into the trees and
disappeared like magic. Turning into my
wolf I headed towards Jaxson's pack to get
ready for our date.
What I hadn't expected was his pack and
Alex's pack to all be waiting for me. Doing
my best to ignore everyone I walked into
Amanda's house to get ready.
When I was finally done I walked outside
and ran straight into Jaxson and her parent's
"So is the council helping us or not?"
"Yes I'll be calling them in a few hours."

"Why so long?"

"I um well I have to go and meet with your daughter."

"But wait didn't use."

"Didn't we what mam?"

"Oh my poor sweet girl."

Amanda's mum leaned into her father and wept.

"It's all going to be alright I promise you."

Amanda's dad held out his hand.

"Son just don't break her heart."

Nodding my head I went to leave but then Jaxson stood in my path. With a nod and a pat on the back he stepped aside. Amanda was really and truly a lucky woman to have all these people. I just hope I could meet their standards.

I managed to finally get into town around dusk. Amanda text me and said she was at a certain restaurant and got a table for two. Finding it I walked inside and expected to see the same casual looking woman I'd just seen this morning.

Instead she came towards me with a long black dress on that showed every curve imaginable. She looked dropped dead gorgeous. I thought she was hot in mum mode but this well damn didn't my cock take notice.

She shyly smiled at me and gave me her hand. Bowing I gently kissed it and then

pulled her towards me and placed a kiss on
her cheek. Her cheeks brightened and her
eyes shone with glee. Placing her arm
around mine I walked us to our table where I
placed her in a chair and then sat in mine.
Overall the night went well; she talked about
the early days of raising Alex, working as a
waitress here in town and how life had been
in Jaxson's pack. She did have a few tears
and I grabbed her hand and rubbed her
knuckles.
She would look at me with hope and despair
but never once did she bring up my leaving.
I told her about all things alpha related.
Sometimes I got shock other times I was
meet with giggles.
She asked about her son's future and I told
her honestly with us together he was going
to be okay. When our meals came we sat
quietly and ate but it was a good silence. We
would just watch each other when the other
wasn't looking.
After the dessert that was when the
atmosphere changed, we were both vibrating
with anticipation. I could smell her arousal a
mile away. Getting up from my chair I went
around and grabbed her hand.
I could see and smell that she wanted this
but she was still very much conflicted.
Kneeling so I was face to face with her I
waited but she said nothing.

"It's okay if you're not ready. They had no right to pressure you."

"It's not that it's just after I don't know if I can."

"It will all work out I promise and I have a few tricks that will help you."

That peeked her curiosity.

"Really like what?"

"Come with me and I will show you."

She did exactly that holding my hand she allowed me to walk her all the way to the edge of town without a word. Stripping down I walked up to her and kissed her on the cheek.

"Come find me."

Winking at her I left before she asked a question. Running some distance I retracted my claws and then climbed a tree. I masked my scent and then pretty much looked down and waited.

It was some time before she managed to get to the spot I was hiding. Watching her I saw her go constantly around in circles and take off in different directions. After some time she decided to just sit.

A breeze picked up and my masked scent traveled to her nostrils. She let out a growl and got to her feet. Looking around she watched and waited for an attack but none came. Deciding enough was enough I jumped out of the tree causing her to yelp.

She looked ready to attack me but I unmasked my alpha scent and allowed her to smell me. I just sat and waited. After a while she yelped again and walked around me. Tail wagging she came to my front literally bopped me on the nose and took off running. I was at a disadvantage now because she knew both my smells so I had to leave everything up to plain old shifter strength. Luckily for me I was faster than your normal alpha. I waited for as long as possible and took off after her. Surely enough I managed to catch her in a clearing. She turned towards me tail wagging. Cade couldn't help himself he dropped and rolled.

"Now is not the time to flirt."

"It is exactly the time."

"No I want to mate her."

"Soon you can do your human thing, but for now this."

He stuck out our tongue and just looked at her upside down. Male wolves really were stupid creatures. However as I watched Amanda lay on her belly and came towards us. Bopping us on the nose again she proceed to lick it.

Well that send Cade bonkers didn't it. He got up and started licking her face all over. For a while she put up with it and then nipped at us. Shocked he rolled on his belly and surrendered to her again.

This caused the she wolf to happily lick our nose and allowed Amanda to return to her human form.

Wrestling control of Cade I finally managed to transform back. When I was I pulled Amanda towards me. Placing my lips on hers I allowed her to take control of the situation. She gently probed me with her tongue until I opened and traced mine along hers. She moaned deep into my mouth and wrapped her arms around my neck.

Wrapping my arms around her I rub my hands all over her.

She felt so curvy and silky smooth it made me groan into her mouth. Grabbing her arse I push her into my erection and wriggle her. After a moment she pulls away and lies on the ground.

"I'm ready."

By god this woman had me by the balls. A drop of pre cum falls from my cock and she eyes it greedily. Shaking my head I drop down to my knees between her legs.

Leaning over her I kiss her mouth and then make a trail to her breasts. Grabbing them both in my hands I lean in and place one nipple in my mouth. Her hands went straight into my hair encouraging me on.

I suck and nibble on one while my other hand twists and pulls the other. She moans and bucks beneath me. She smelt divine like forests and something sweet that I couldn't place. Popping her nipple out of my mouth I move to the other.

After a while she started begging me to fuck her but I just couldn't. Licking and nipping my way down to her body I kiss her mound but I don't go inside not just yet.

I trail kisses all the way down to her knees, kiss her mound and then do the same thing on the other side. By now she is wriggling and I can see she's dripping wet.

I blow some air on her pussy making her shiver. Very, very slowly I lick her from the bottom all the way to the top. She groans out loud and grabs my head. Spreading her lips slightly I flick my tongue inside and I'm surrounded by her arousal and smell.

Almost losing control I wrap my hand around my cock and give it a pull. Groaning into her pussy causes her to push closer towards me.

Any closer and I was going to drown she was just that wet. Not like it would have been a bad way to die but still. Moving my mouth away I place one and then two fingers inside her. She yells out loud and then stays pushing on my hand.

I wanted to draw this out but I could see she was so close.

I begin moving my fingers inside her and before long she's lost all control. She's pulling my hair, screaming for me to go faster and rubbing her face like she was going crazy.

I move in and nip on her clit and that takes her over the edge. Her thighs clamp around me and she screams my name. When she goes limp I crawl over her and look at her face.

Her hair was a mess however those lazy eyes are what captivated me they were so sparkly and bright. It was almost like there was love there. Leaning down I kiss her gently.

Grabbing my cock I place it at her entrance and enter her slowly. She let out little moans and grabbed onto my arm. By the time I fully seated inside I was breathing quite heavily. She was so wet and so tight it took everything not to cum.

"Are you going to move?"

"Just give me a minute."

"Has it been a while?"

"You could say that."

She wraps a hand around my neck and pulls me down for a kiss. Getting lost in her taste and smell I begun to move: It was pure love making. Slow and steady, in and out. A stolen kiss here a foot in the butt there: After a time her orgasm must have built again because she dug both feet into my arse and pushed against me. I however was not rushing this. She wanted me to love her and that was exactly what I was doing.

Her movements below me were becoming more frantic she was chasing the high. Watching her chase it I couldn't take it no longer. I thrusted into her with everything I had.

As our movements became more frantic I felt the tingle in my balls letting me know I was close. I moved a hand between us and pinched her clit.

With her screaming my name again I pounded into her until I found my own release and dropped.

So as not to squish her I leaned on my elbows and kissed her eyes, her nose and finally her mouth.

She lazily smiled up at me and turned her neck. This was it, this was the moment I had been waiting for. One bite and she was mine forever. Leaning over her I placed a kiss to her neck and then bit down on her shoulder.

She screamed out loud with her pussy clenching around me automatically causing both of us to come again.

Releasing her I look down to see the area is already healing. I kiss her neck and roll off pulling her into my arms. I knew what tomorrow was going to bring but for now I had a new mate and if memory serves a baby on the way.

Chapter Ten

Amanda

I woke in Lachlan's arms in the middle of nowhere. Smiling I lift my head and he looked down at me smiling. We did it we were mates for life and him being a greater alpha it looked like a long life indeed.

Then it dawned on me and my smile faded to nothing. Today was the day I'd get my son back and my mate may just have to leave me.

Getting up so he wouldn't see me cry I told him we had to get back to the pack.

Leaving him stunned in the clearing I allowed Casey to take over my body and we set off.

"It will be okay."

"You don't know that."

"I'm sure he will be allowed to keep in contact."

"That might be true but it still hurts."

When a mate went on a mission there could be no contact for several days and even weeks. It was to protect the pack from humans and those that wanted to harm us.

Running faster than I thought possible I managed to get back to Jaxson's territory in no time at all. Heading to the stay houses

I'm met by my son's whole pack. Changing into my human form I talk to them.

"Right is everyone ready to go?"

"We are sweetie but where is that Marcus and Lachlan?"

"We're here and we're ready. I'll carry Marcus on my back."

"Why can't he just transform?"

"He's our secret weapon."

"Rightio everyone ready then?"

"Let's go get our kids back."

Everyone transformed into their wolves and set off.

"Hello mate I'm Cade."

Stopping in my tracks I pushed Casey to the front of my mind. I couldn't deal with my mate or his wolf right now.

"I am Casey."

"Such a pretty name for a pretty wolf."

Lachlan tried to bring me into their conversation however I was not interested. My mind had to stay on point or I would just fall apart.

We stalked for many miles until Marcus got a call telling him Elijah and the wolves were resting in the states national park. Relieved we all picked up the pace. If we were lucky and didn't have a break we would be there by lunchtime tomorrow.

We ran throughout the night only stopping to hunt and drink. By the time we got close enough all the wolves were exhausted so we had no choice but to set up camp. Everyone transformed back and set camp up around dawn. Unable to sleep I just sat at the campfire watching the sparks just float away.

Lachlan came to sit with me and said I needed rest but I shook off his concern.

He walked away and transformed into his wolf. Sitting alone I curled into myself and eventually started to cry. This was it our babies were coming home.

What left me mourning was what would happen after. Lachlan and I had magically fallen hard and soon he was to leave me.

Several hours later Lachlan came back and there was a smile on his face.

"What are you so happy about?"

"I did surveillance and I'm happy to report those wolves haven't moved."

"That's a good thing?"

"Actually yes your little alpha is none too impressed."

I sat shocked how much drama could a little toddler be?

"His wolf refuses to transform and when he does well let's just say he will make you and his father proud."

A tear slowly rolled down my face. I have always been proud of my son but in this moment I felt like my heart would explode.

He was indeed my son, a fighter in the making.

"So can we go?"

"Are you sure you don't need rest?"

"I am totally sure."

"What about…?"

"I'm barely pregnant I know there's a risk but Casey and the pack will protect me."

"Alright then."

Lachlan woke everyone up and as soon as they were it felt like an electrical current went through the camp. Everyone was hot wired and I was sure ready to kill. Marcus climbed on Lachlan's back and we set off. Running as fast as we could but not so fast the rest of the pack couldn't keep up we got to their camp within three hours.

The plan was simple everyone would separate the rouges from Elijah who we were sure had the kids.

Howls broke out and the fight begun. Lachlan and I had to fight our way through a few wolves but we were an amazing team. Back to back we were toe to toe with those mongrels' and before long we were faced with Elijah.

"Mumma."

Hearing my son was a relief however Elijah looked like he was planning our deaths. Growling I stood my ground ready to attack however my son had other plans. He transformed and went straight for Elijah's leg. Trying to shake my son off I went to go in however he booted my son across clearing and transformed.

"Mate go to your son. Marcus and I have this."

Nodding my head I slowly kept an eye on Elijah as I made my way to my son. He growled at me and I barked back. I had to trust my mate. I made it to Alex unharmed, bending down I nudged him with our nose. He lifted his head and yipped.

Licking him I told him we had to get his friend. He got up but fell to the group yelping. Whimpering he showed me his paw. I looked to Lachlan.

"Alpha or not kill the bastard he hurt our son."

Lachlan nodded his head and attacked Elijah. Looking back down at my son I picked him up by the collar. Slowly making our way around we managed to get to Alex's beta that was in pup mode barking his head off. Once he noticed us he came towards us and I put his alpha down.

He nudged my son and laid beside him watching the battle unfold. This time Elijah and Lachlan where evenly matched however I noticed something was off, Marcus was gone.

Looking around I couldn't see him anywhere, a shadow appeared over us. Looking up I saw nothing. Looking back down at the males I see Lachlan take a hit. I pounced up ready to help however he told me to stand back. Watching in horror I see Elijah ram Lachlan into a tree and he falls to the ground. He turned towards the pups and I … but then something horrifying happened.

Elijah was lifted from the ground by an invisible force. A sudden roar went around the forest stopping every wolf in their tracks. Elijah was trying to scratch and bite his way free but it was of no use. Higher and higher he went until the invisible force dropped him.

He was falling at a dramatic speed. When he hit the ground he crumpled into a heap. Another thud hit the ground a second later. Right before my eyes a massive black dragon appeared. It picked Elijah up by the throat instantly breaking his neck.

The dragon dropped him roared again and then started to transform. After a moment Marcus stood where the dragon had been. He turned and smiled at me and then went to Lachlan.

A bloody dragon are you serious? They're meant to be creatures of myths and legends.

So much was running through my mind but I was frozen in shock. Marcus and Lachlan embraced and then he turned, transformed and left. Looking at Lachlan with what I assumed was a weird look on my face he began to laugh.

Snapping out of it I growled at him. The boys transformed back into little humans and began talking about dinosaurs.

Needing answers I asked Casey to transform back which she was more than happy to. Running into Lachlan's arms he was still laughing.

"That was a bloody dragon."

"Yep."

"How is that possible?"

"Dragons have been around for a long time."

"Yes but…"

"They were hunted to the point of extinction however they hid the remaining females and allowed their   numbers to multiply. Marcus is one of the oldest."

"A bloody dragon no one will believe me."

"And so they shouldn't."

"What about the boys?"

"Children have great imaginations don't worry in time they will forget."

Nodding my head I leaned up to kiss Lachlan and then turned and picked up the boys. It was finally over we could go home. All the pack members came to us and I gave

Melissa her son. Her son transformed and they both began yipping and yapping in joy.
"Oh no Damien's mate where is she?"
"Don't worry Marcus took care of them, they're fine."
Nodding my head I watched as my new pack rejoiced with having there alpha and beta returned. When we left it took several days to return home and to our surprise the supreme council was waiting. I asked Melissa to take the boys inside and walked to them with Lachlan.
"We held up the end of the bargain now it is your turn."
"Please just some time with my family?"
"Fine but when you feel the pull you must leave."
"I promise sir thank you."
The council walked away and Lachlan wrapped me in his arms. I was grateful we had time but just how much. Over the coming days a few stray wolves told us what Elijah had said and done. In the end we found out the council members were just frighten of Elijah however it was too late they were gone.
Many wolves sort forgiveness but were handed over to the council. To them kidnapping was not okay.

There was one other council member out there however he surprised us by asking for a meeting.

He swore he had no part in anything and asked for forgiveness. Lachlan allowed him to stay around to prove he was no threat. When Lachlan was satisfied the other member seemed to be no threat he allowed him to leave.

For several days after the boys were surrounded by the pack to ensure their safety. When Lachlan was sure he wouldn't return he made a judgment call. Taking me outside away from the boys he laid down the law.

"These boys need discipline and they need social activity."

"But what if?"

"No buts Amanda."

"But…"

"NO BUTS they need to be with children their own age."

"Alright I'll take them to the pack school tomorrow."

"Thank you I…" Lachlan groaned and then let out a growl.

"What is it?"

"An alpha has come to be I must go."

"NO… I WONT LET YOU."

"It is the deal I made I must go."

He walked up to me holding me in an
embrace. With tears streaming down my
face I held onto him tightly. He placed a
finger under my chin and placed but a single
kiss on my lips.
Casey howled in my mind causing Cade to
fight Lachlan. He bent over holding his
head. I could see the turmoil this was
causing my mate so I did the only thing I
could do.
I got on my knees and put my face to his, I
prayed Casey would understand.
"LEAVE."
Cade stopped fighting Lachlan who
appeared shocked.
"Leave or I will renounce the mate claim."
Casey howled in my mind, holding my head
high I ignored her and push forth.
"GO NOW."
Lachlan looked at me heartbroken but
nodded his head once and turned into a wolf.
Turning my back on them both I walked
away and then stopped.
"I was a single mother before I can do it
again." I turned back around and they were
gone.
"I'm sorry Casey it had to be done."
"You won't really renounce them will you?"
"Of course not they will return if not for us
for the children."

As she wailed in my mind a howl filled the forest. He wasn't dead but with the heartache I felt he may as well of been. I walked inside to where the boys were with Melissa.

She looked towards me with a smile however seeing my looked rushed towards us and wrapped us in her arms. I broke down and cried.

That night Melissa stayed with me and I told her what Lachlan said before he left. She reluctantly agree however when we got to the school the next day she totally agreed with him.

The boys took off at once and began playing with the other children like the past few weeks hadn't happened. Sure they were still talking about dinosaurs but we just laughed it off.

It seemed everything was right in the world. All accept me and my broken heart.

In time the supreme council came back to us and stated we had to go to their territory for the boy's sake. In reality they were right our pack didn't belong here but where did we belong?

With a lot of tears and hugs goodbye to Jaxson's pack we all set off with a possibility of a permanent home and a brand new life with our boys. Many of the members tried to make us feel welcome and encouraged the boys to hunt along the way. It was a tireless journey especially with two toddlers however when we finally got there everyone stood in amazement. There were animals of all shapes and breeds and to the boys delight dragons.

The members showed us our new living arrangements and to our surprise it was exactly like what we had at Jaxson's but grander.

"There you guys are we were expecting you two days ago."

"I um sorry Marcus the kids."

"No need to apologize come."

The other members fell away and allowed Marcus to show us around. My new home was the biggest out of the others surrounding it. It was fully furnished and that included a room for the baby. I smiled in delight but my mind shut down. Even though this was our home it wasn't home without Lachlan.

"I know what you're thinking but he will be back soon enough."

"How can you be so sure?"

"He's reported in and sent three baby greater alphas our way and their families."

"Really but he's only been gone a short while."

"Well I guess you wolves breed like rabbits come let's get your family settled."
Over the next couple of weeks we all settled into our new homes. The boys got put into school and the whole pack finally got the chance to relax. Melissa had finally given in to Simon and was pregnant.

I was really, really happy for them as we could raise all the children together again. However when the nights came I was all alone.
Alex picked up on the moods and started acting up not just at home but also at school. Raising a child was hard enough without that child being as special as Alex is.

Chapter Eleven

Amanda

"ROLL."

"NO."

"ROLL."

"STOP IT."

"Mummy roll NOW."

Shaking and unable to keep standing due to his power Casey rolled. Whimpering in my mind I knew how she felt. Alex was becoming more and more complicated to manage.

Without Lachlan here to put him in his place myself and the pack were suffering. It actually got to the point I had to stop school and there were no more sleepovers with my parents.

"SHAKE."

Casey did exactly what he asked. This went on for half an hour before a knock finally came at the door. Alex's eyes stopped glowing and Casey collapsed to the floor.

Alex walked off like nothing had happened. Shaking I managed to get us to all fours and then transform. Getting dressed I went to answer the door.

"Marcus what are you doing here?"

"I came to see how you're doing. The pack said you disappeared."

"Of course they did come in I'll put the kettle on."
As he walked in the door an excited Alex ran up to
him. Seeing it was Marcus he got angry. Eye's
glowing he stood up to the older alpha.
With the battle of minds going on in the lounge
room Casey and I began to quiver, the power was
frightening. After a minute or two Alex stood down.
Running off to his room he slammed the door and
started crying.
"What, what happened?"
"Being so young it could be many things."
"I know I thought about going to a council."
"That could be an idea but that won't fix the
problem."
"Then what will?"
"My guess is he needs another alpha around."
"Lachlan?"
He nodded his head. It was like I was struck by
lightning. Of course it was Lachlan. Why hadn't I
thought of that? Yes Casey and I were suffering but
Alex had to be as well. Lachlan had come in at the
beginning of our journey.
Alex must have seen him as a father figure or role
model. Putting my head in my hands I broke down
and begun to cry. Marcus went to get up to do
whatever but stopped.
"It's okay, I'm okay."
"No you're not."
"What would you have me do? I can't beg him to
come home."

"Take the boy hunting, put him into school and keep to a routine. I promise it will get easier."

"Yes but when?"

"I cannot tell you."

Nodding my head I watched as Marcus looked towards Alex door and then left. Marcus was right I didn't have a male in my life before and we did just fine. I just had to make my son see the exact same thing. Going to his bedroom door I knocked.

"GO AWAY."

Trying to not buckle under the pressure I opened the door. Eyes shining Alex looked straight at me.

"I know you miss Lachlan I do too."

"No I don't."

"Well how about we go get some rabbits?"

That did the trick. He popped straight into his puppy form and ran out the door barking. Smiling I let out a sigh. Grabbing my keys off the counter I opened the door and walked outside with my alpha.

Yipping and yapping he barreled down the stairs and into the pen. Locking him in I go over to the yard where we kept the rabbits and pulled the biggest one out.

Walking over to the pen I drop it in with Alex and go and sit on the step. Both the rabbit and Alex did nothing for several moments. The rabbit sensing danger took a hop to the side and Alex bounced. Running around chasing the rabbit I felt the power come off him in waves.

It was uncomfortable to feel but it was tolerable. He eventually managed to get his paws on the rabbit but he let it go.

He growled and then went chasing it again. On and on this went until Alex was tired out and flopped on the ground. I got up to get him out of the pen however his eyes glowed and then he turned his back on me.

Sitting back down I just quietly waited and watched. Suddenly an adorable howl filled the air. I smiled however Casey pushed forth in my mind causing a transformation.

Letting out her own howl Alex looked towards us. Neither of us moving Alex howled again Casey joining him. This wasn't your pack howl, this was mourning, grief, loss. They were howling for Lachlan. When they were all howled out I managed to transform back and go to my son. His fur was tear stricken and he was whimpering.

"I know baby I know I'm so sorry."

That night Alex didn't eat, he snuggled up to me in his wolf form and went to sleep. The next day I woke up early and surprisingly Alex was still in his wolf form. Getting out of bed I went to make coffee and breakfast.

When he finally came out he was in human form. Looking at the table he got so excited he popped in and out of pup form. I couldn't help but smile.

"If you keep doing that you're not going to be able to eat come on."

Yipping at me he transformed back and sat at the
table. Munching on his food he asked if he could go
to school. I pondered the situation until a knock
came at the door. Going to answer it, it was Melissa
and her son. Inviting them in her son goes to sit
with mine and they both chow down on the food.
Both Melissa and I laughed.
"Today looks like a good day."
"Don't jinx it it's just begun."
After the boys finished eating we got them ready
and off we all went to school. Dropping them off
Melissa and I headed back home. Telling her I
would see her this afternoon I went home and
climbed back into bed.
Finally managing to drift off I dreamed of the final
day Lachlan was home. Waking up in tangled
sheets Casey whimpered in my mind. Getting out of
bed I go around the house cleaning up until I had to
get Alex.
Over the coming few months we got into the routine
of hunting, school and allowing our wolves to howl
into the nothing. It seemed like a normal healthy
routine until bedtime one night. I had managed to
get to the second trimester of my pregnancy without
drama and the baby started kicking.
Alex had been lying on my stomach when the baby
kicked.
Looking at my stomach in a confused head tilt he
just stared at it. After a moment he laid back down
but the baby kicked again. This time he growled and

yipped at my stomach. Laughing at him he looked at me dumbfounded.

"That's your baby brother or sister."

He yipped at me. Smiling at him I patted his head and told him about the baby, however when I got to Lachlan being the daddy he laid down on my stomach and whimpered. Silent tears ran down my face.

We hadn't talked about Lachlan for a while as it was a trigger for him, however this time there was no anger just sadness.

Afterward we added baby cuddles into the picture. I put a sonogram picture in his room so he could get the understanding however it was hard to comprehend. I did however notice a huge change in Alex's behavior. He stopped forcing me to change and commanding me around. Instead he went into big brother mode without thinking. He would command the pack to not come near us and would not leave my side.

In many ways this was a good thing but it was also bad. Casey had become isolated and wouldn't allow the change. Every wolf needed pack and also the hunt but for her it was all about the kids. Alex had managed to get Casey to come out on a few occasions but even he stopped asking.

Weeks turned into months and before long the baby had arrived. Surprisingly it was a girl. Both Alex and Casey were excited. We all stayed hold up in the house. There were plenty of tears, laughter and joy.

Alex loved feeding his baby sister and just being with her. On many occasions I had to remind him that he was a wolf and he also had the pack. People came by however Alex refused entry.

I was actually okay with it but I knew the pack was paying the price. Two months after Lily was born Melissa had her baby a boy. We went to the hospital to see the new pack member.

Everyone had plenty of cuddles and plenty of puppy kisses from our alpha and beta. Looking at Melissa I smiled but our joy was short lived. Our alpha and beta ended up in full pack mode. Melissa and I were constantly being woken by the boys when our babies were in distress. It got worse and worse as the babies got older.

The boys stayed in wolf form a lot as the babies started to crawl. Melissa and I had to force the children apart as they called on the pack for protection when it wasn't necessary. One occasion Alex pulled Lily away from the TV via the suit. That was actually pretty cute and funny.

On other occasions one of the babies would fall and hurt themselves and the boys would just go mental. Casey relished in the peace and quiet. No longer a betas mate and Alex in big brother mode she was able to hide. It hurt but I know she was mourning for her mate.

One night Lily woke up screaming. Running to her room I already found Alex in there. Shaking my head I picked up my daughter and took her to the lounge room. Sitting down rocking her Alex watched at my feet. Though she settled she was still restless and refused to go back to sleep. I got up and a sudden buzzing noise filled my head.

Before I knew it I was in wolf form. Casey walked us over to the children and just sat. Alex transformed back and talked to his sister.

"Lily, Lily it's okay look."

"Puppy roll."

Before I could do anything Casey laid down and rolled. My daughter started clapping her hands. Casey rolled the other way and then barked. Alex commanded us to roll, sit, play dead and fetch and Casey did everything asked.

I watched in complete silence as my daughter and son connected on a new level. And so began playtime with mummy puppy. Alex being an alpha would play peek a boo popping in an out of pup form but it was him commanding.

Casey and I that brought real joy to my children's faces. When his sister started walking that had its own complications. Alex would sneak her into the pen indicating he wanted to show her to hunt however I refused as she was too busy cuddling the rabbits. Alex already had issues I didn't need another child having issues as well.

Due to my children bonding and having Casey back in the picture we begun to really live. Sure I was sad without Lachlan but I knew he would be here if he could. Alex allowed the whole pack to come together which entertainingly enough made not only Lily happy but Melissa's son as well. It was like wolf pack yoga. Every day after school all the older pack members would come together and do tricks to entertain the children.

What always brought a smile to my face was they would have several of my sons pack members going around in circles chasing their friggen tails. It was alright for us younger wolves but my folks struggled.

They would fall over; bump into each or just straight up look like drunk wolves. The children would laugh, clap and scream out again, again. It was good to see my children working and bringing us all together.

However things changed towards Lilies second birthday and Alex was none to impressed. We had all been outside and Lily randomly pops into pup form. Freaking out everyone ran towards her. It only meant one thing the pack had another greater alpha.

Lily freaking out was yipping, yapping and chasing her tail. I picked her up and though she growled there was no power coming from her. I handed her over to my parents, Melissa, Simon and even the others that had alpha children.

Not once did her eyes glow and not once did any of the children move to claim her. We were all at a loss.

It wasn't until Melissa's son was turning two that all hell broke loose. It turned out Melissa's son was one of the greater alphas that Lachlan was searching for. What was confusing was Lily gravitated towards him. It wasn't the bond of a beta and alpha but it wasn't fully pack member behavior either. It meant only two things they were too young to create the bond or they were future mates, neither thought was pleasing. For once in my adult life couldn't I have had a normal child?

Alex didn't like the fact at all that his baby sister was owned by another and this caused a lot of in house fighting. Alex being bigger would fight Melissa's son for dominance but it was like a game of cat and mouse. Neither child would submit as they were too evenly matched. In the end we had to separate the children.

It was worse for Melissa as one of her children was an Alpha, the other the beta to my son.

Most days were full of tears while other days we managed some sort of life. When things got hard I begged and begged for Lachlan to come home.

Not to be my mate but to sort out this fiasco we called our lives. On one of our good days we were all outside just watching the children having fun chasing their tails when Marcus popped up out of nowhere.

"Hi, what are you doing here?"

"Just came to check in."

"Oh well no need as you can see."

"I do, it seems they're in good hands."

"For now come back tomorrow." We both laughed and watched the children."

"Lachlan is coming home."

With a wink he disappeared. I looked to my pack members and those that joined us due to their children. There were smiles and also silent tears. Casey yipped in my mind. I knew how she felt soon very soon we were going to be in the arms of our mate and he can sort out this mess he left us with.

Chapter Twelve

Lachlan

Almost two friggen years of constantly traveling, constantly infiltrating packs to find the last two greater alphas. I managed to find the first three no problems at all, their parents more than willing to go to council lands and get their children the much needed help they needed.

But here I was just chasing my tail around in circles. Cade had stopped talking to me completely so I was in this alone.

Some nights I would howl to the moon with no mourning call back. In the beginning Cade would force us to our mate but I had to reinforce what our mate said.

I didn't know if it was true but it still cut deep just the same. I was missing both her and Alex the same. Her words from the day they were kidnapped running through my mind.

"He hurt our son."

Not her son our son, the words where torture. And it wasn't just them now I imagined she had given birth by now. Was it a boy? Or did I have a daughter? It was unknown. Every time I rung the council with updates I wouldn't get an answer they

wanted me focused on this mission, a
mission that seemed endless. Two greater
alphas should have been born by now but
they weren't.

Getting back into my human form again
failing to reconnect with Cade I find my
nearest pub and drown my sorrows. I ended
many countless searches like this.
Always drinking and then sleeping in wolf
form or finding my closest hotel. After a few
drinks a pretty young woman walks up to
me and asks for a drink. Cade finally taking
notice growls in my mind.
"I'll pass thanks."
She lays a hand on my arm and Cade loses
it.
"Push her away she isn't our mate."
"What do you think I'm doing?"
"Excuse me?" Shit I had spoken out loud.
"Look your pretty but I am not interested."
"Come on just one drink."
""MAKE HER LEAVE OR I WILL BITE
HER."
Shit this was bad very bad I couldn't wolf
out here in the bar. I quickly push off my
chair and walk to the exit. The little hot
thing tried to follow us. I turned around to
tell her off but she must have seen
something in my face and cowered away.
Walking as fast as I could as Cade was just
below the surface I just managed to make it

to the woods. Unable to control the shift he took over and took off.

For several days he wouldn't allow us to change back. He would eat and only slept when he knew I was asleep. By the fifth day he finally came around.

He understood that I didn't want that female but was still angry that she touched us. I was worn out, tired and hungry. He allowed us to transform back so we could get nutrients and continue the search.

After resting we took off again it finally happened I felt the pull. I ran around frantic for a while as it kept going on and off like a beacon but when I got the strongest pull I was surprised where I ended up. I ended back up in Redwater and Jaxson was none too surprised to see me.

"You bloody greater alphas."

"WHERE IS HE?"

"Easy he's this way come."

I followed him to his house where a frightened female and male sat waiting.

"Where is your child?"

"He's, he's…"

Out came a little pup with a shoe in his mouth. It would have been hilarious however I was just thinking of the end goal. One more to go and I could go home. The pup dropped the shoe and growled at me. Growling back at the child he raced to his mother's side where she picked him up. I looked to his parents and spoke.

"I'm not here to take your child."

"We know."

"Okay well you must leave, here is a number to call to get you to the council lands."

"What about the wolf council can't we stay there?"

"The wolf council is no more for the time being Amanda will help you."

"Oh my god Amanda I remember her."

"Yes she will help you now go."

They nodded their heads thanks and I went outside. I was hoping to call Marcus with an update but Jaxson followed me outside.

"How is Amanda?"

"Well as far as I know."

"What do you mean as far as you know?"

"I haven't seen her in nearly two years."

"WHAT…"

"Hey it's not what you think."

I didn't get a chance to elaborate as Jaxson's fist connected with my face. I growled at him but did nothing more.

"You have some explaining to do."

"I don't have to explain myself to you."

"Amuse me then."

"Or what?"

"I could just beat it out of you."

Sighing I ran a hand through my hair and sat on the ground. Cade was pissed a lower alpha hit us but it was nothing compared to the pain he felt missing Casey and Amanda.

"I made a deal with the supreme council."

"What kind of deal?"

"I would hunt down the next greater alphas and then return home."

"What about Amanda?"

"She let us go."

"SHE DID WHAT?"

"She let us go, she had no choice."

"But the children? What about what happened last time she lost a mate did you not think about that?"

"IT'S ALL I'VE THOUGHT ABOUT."

"Well…"

"Well what?"

"How many children have you left to find?"

"Just one."

"What are you sitting around here for go find it? Two years is a long time without a mate."

"Don't you think I know that?"

"Well go NOW."

I looked up at Jaxson and he offered me his hand. Taking it I stood up.

"I'm sorry I hit you."

"I deserved it."

He placed a hand on my shoulder and with a nod of his head he left me alone. I got my

phone out to ring Marcus. On the third ring
he picked up.

"Oh man so glad you called."

"Yeah well I have some news."

"Well what is it?"

"I found the forth greater alpha you
wouldn't believe where I found it."

"Come man don't keep me waiting."

"It was in Redwater."

"Man for a small pack they pack a punch.
Do you want to hear my good news?"

"If you're going to say Ellen is pregnant
again that's not surprising you fuck like
rabbits."

We both had a laugh but what he said next
shocked me.

"You can come home my friend."

"But I haven't found the last alpha."

"The council said to come home that is all I
can say."

Marcus hung up the phone and I looked at it
shocked and then Cade's excitement took
over my body we were going home. I raced
inside and told the new alphas family that I
would personally be taking them to their
new home.

Though they were reluctant they allowed me
to escort them. The pup picking up on my
vibe came bouncing over and I picked him
up.

Allowing the little creature to lick my face his golden eyes shone into mine. Cade seeing the command did the same to mine causing the pup to yelp. The mother came flying over and I laughed.

"He's okay I was just letting him know whose boss."

"But aren't you a greater alpha too?"

"For now but when I get home I will be sworn in as the greater alpha for the supreme council."

"So when do we leave?"

"As soon as you're ready, don't worry about your things a new house and belongings await you."

It took several hours and many, many goodbyes but we were finally off home and to my new family. Every now and then I had to remind Cade to slow down as these wolves not only had a child but they weren't as fast as us. While we were traveling I showed the little alpha how to hunt just as Amanda did with Alex.

There were many laughs and many worried looks from the parents however the journey had been pretty smooth sailing. When we got to council land we were met by the council. Marcus came to me with a big embrace.

"Welcome home old friend."

"Where is Amanda? Where are the children?"

"In time, in time, for now come."

Nodding my head I watched as some members took the wolf family to their new home. No one said anything until we were in some sort of building.

I was told to be seated however I was practically on vibrate.

"You must excuse my rudeness."

"That is understandable alpha. Now we called you home as you have held up the end of your bargain. We understand the torment you went through."

"You understand nothing."

"Perhaps, perhaps now there is something you need to do before you go home."

"Yes, what, anything!"

"You must join the council."

"Is that it?"

"For now there is one more member to replace you, now come."

I walked around the room to the member of the council and stopped in my tracks. I'd never been this close to him before now and be damned if I wasn't shocked. He was a dragon.

I looked around the room towards Marcus who happily smiled and then said in my mind to bow. Not knowing what I was agreeing to I did exactly that. He placed a hand on my head.

"I Rothman king of the dragons and the supernatural community proclaim this greater alpha to be a member of the supreme council. Do you swear your loyalty to the council and no one but the council?

Do you swear to still uphold our laws and carry out justice if a greater alpha steps out of line including your own son?"

If I said no I was going to be banned, stripped or forsaken but could I really kill Amanda's son if he went rouge?

Cade growled in my head but I had to calm him or god knows what was going to happen us. Amanda and the kids were too important. Swallowing my pride and my fatherly duties I agreed.

A sudden power washed over me, it felt warm and welcoming like I was where I was meant to be. However the feeling quickly faded and I remembered why I had come. I was just about to see my family.

"Thank you your highness but I don't mean to be rude…"

"Yes go son I'm sure they will be happy to see you."

I all but ran out the door. The wolves were easy to find but what shocked me was there wasn't two pups on my door but several. All the pups looked towards me and growled.

All of them had golden eyes except two which meant the last alpha had been here all along but whose was it?

"They can sense you but they can't see you."

Marcus popped out of nowhere giving me a fright.

"What do you mean I'm right here?"

"Indeed however your invisible, one of the perks of being on the council."

"How did that happen?"

"Until you train to use it, it will happen when your emotions go through the roof."

"How do I appear?"

"Not for some time I'm afraid as you're in for one hell of a homecoming."

Laughing he walked off leaving me jumping out of my boots and thoroughly confused. Following behind him I watched as he interacted with the new wolf members and sat down and played with the pups. I was going to go in search of my mate but low and behold she came walking outside. She looked like an angel.

My heart pounded a hundred mile a second. I'd have given anything to appear and hold her. However that was not the case she walked over to the pups, shocking me she picked two of them up.

Taking them away from the group I followed her. She walked them to a huge house and sat them on the ground. The bigger of the pups transformed and to no surprise it was Alex.

Quietly watching the scene unfold I watched how my mate undressed. It felt like yesterday that I got to see all those luscious curves but it was the look in her eyes that broke me.

Though my dick was rock hard I stood quietly as it appeared a lesson was being learned here. She transformed into Casey and before my eyes the other pup transformed back.

I completely dropped to the ground shock. The wolf wasn't just a greater alpha but he was in fact a she. She looked towards Alex and said roll mummy roll. Alex's eye's shone and sure enough Casey rolled.

Happily the little girl squealed and yelled again, again.

This went on for several moments. Every time Alex commanded a new trick Casey did exactly what he said. Though this was abuse of power I did not put my foot down. It seemed Casey was more than happy to follow the commands.

It was in that moment I also realized she wasn't the greater alpha. I had more questions than answers at that point but I had to become visible to get them. As looking at my family's joy was keeping me in this state what could I do to get out of it. That's when it hit me, all those lonely nights without my family, not being able to feel my mates belly as she grew big and round. The haunted look in her eyes before she transformed.

That must have done the trick because Alex turned his head towards me. Sending out a command to leave, I sent out one to stand down and the poor kid nearly buckled. Running towards him to help I was stopped by a very pissed off she-wolf. Well I thought she was pissed because the next second she was on top of me licking me to death. Cade lost his friggen mind and forced our transformation.

Not that I could blame him Casey was all over him like a bad smell. Licking, yipping and allowing these two to reconnect I reached out to Amanda but there was no answer. I knew she would be in shock so I just let it go.

The kids picked up on the excitement and transformed themselves. Before I knew it we were all running around chasing each other and just enjoining the moment.

Before long it was all over and Casey transformed into Amanda. Picking up the female pup she begged Alex to transform and to come inside however he was squaring off with me. Eye's glowing I could see the turmoil within them. He may have only been two when I left but part of him remembered. Not giving it a second though he charged at me. Not knowing the full extent of my powers I was behind him in a second.

"Don't hurt him he's just upset."

I nodded my head and waited for the little alpha to make the next move. In the end it was a game of cat and mouse. I understood the child's feelings but this was going to solve nothing.

In the end I allowed him a cheap shot. He grabbed a hold of my leg viciously shaking. He drew blood however there was no pain, my heart just broke for the boy.

Amanda came and wrestled him off my leg. He was snapping and growling but not once did he demand that she put him down. I didn't know if it was his wolf or because of his mother, either way I was grateful. I stayed outside until nightfall. When I knew both the children were asleep I transformed back and quietly knocked on the door.

Chapter Thirteen

Amanda

Once I managed to get both the children inside I placed Alex down and he transformed back. His sister on the other was running around wildly squealing that daddy was home.

Alex just death stared me and walked to his room. Slamming the door shut he left me with his sister alone. Alex was a handful indeed but he had nothing compared to this little energy bunny.

She was running loops around me while I was trying to dress her.

I understood her excitement as my mate her dad had come home as he said he would. My heart however broke for my son. Before Lachlan left the boys had gotten quite close and now that connection was gone.

Finally managing to get my daughter dressed I went to knock on Alex's door but he told me to go away. Leaving him be I curled up on the lounge with my daughter and watched cartoons.

Hours later I got dinner ready and Alex came out of his room. I tried to strike up a conversation with him but nothing. He ate and then went to bed. My daughter on the other hand was a mini cyclone.

She was so excited at seeing her dad she wanted to see him again. If she didn't settle down soon I'd have to go next door and get her alpha and possible mate. God that thought filled me with dread what was Lachlan going to say to that.

Finally managing to get her to lie down I read stories about fairy gardens and princesses until she finally fell asleep. Creeping out of her room I shut the door. Now I was alone and Casey was filling me with sexual energy.

I understood her frustration but I didn't even know where Lachlan was, I sure as hell wasn't having sex right not with Alex out of control. Unable to leave I sat on the lounge. An hour or two must of past before a knock came at the door.

Slowly I made my way to the door and opened it. Right before my eyes Lachlan stood in all his sexy glory. The sexual tension intensified and it took everything in me to reel it in. I invited him in and we went into the lounge room. Sitting at opposite ends we just sat quietly looking at each other.

"You know Cade is yelling for me to fuck you right."

"I know so is Casey."

"So what is the problem?"

"The children."

"Yes of course I apologize."

"It's okay now your home."

"How have you been?"

"It's been hard I'm not going to lie."

"And the children?"

"They're amazing Alex has come leaps and bounds and Lily?"

"Lily after your mother."

"I, yes I hope you don't mind."

"Of course not."

"When can I actually meet her?"

"Whenever you want but you need to think about Alex."

"Of course he has been through a lot."

"He has when you left..."

"I know and I am so sorry."

"It's not your fault."

"I know but I just left without even saying goodbye."

"I'm sure he will come around."

"Maybe."

"Are you not even going to ask?"

"Ask what?"

"Why your daughter is a wolf but not an alpha."

"I have to admit I was shocked to see but…"

"She's tied to Melissa's son."

He looked at me shocked and I couldn't help but laugh.

"Not Alex's beta her other son."

"So that's who the last alpha was."

"Yes but we don't know how."

"What do you mean?"

"Well she turned before he turned and there different."

"Please don't say it."

He groaned and placed his head in his hands.

"There is a high chance she is his mate."

"I was afraid you were going to say that."

I admit I was shocked when we all figured it out but for a first time dad and to a female no less I guess it was a lot of information. For the rest of the night we caught up on everything Lachlan and Cade missed out on. Some of it had him laughing his head off while a lot of it had grief rolling off him. Around dawn I had no choice but to ask him to leave, the children would be awake soon and I didn't want another scene like yesterday.

I walked him to the door, I felt my heartbreak but I reminded myself this wasn't permanent. He stepped outside and turned to me. He raised his hand but had second thoughts about it.

He went to leave but I forced him to face me one last time. Wrapping my arms around him I placed a kiss on his lips. Wrapping his arms around me he took the kiss deeper and before I knew it I was seeing stars.

Letting me go he promised he was going to hang around. Nodding my head I close the door.

That kiss was ten times better than the last one, it made my nipples hard and my lady parts tingle. Taking some deep breaths I got everything ready for the day. By the time the children woke their bags were packed and a huge breakfast waited for them.

After yesterday's surprise visit I managed some small talk with the children. Alex looked glum but he was happy to be seeing his best friend and beta. Once everyone was good to go I grabbed their bags and got them out the door.

I could sense Lachlan however I couldn't see him. Shyly smiling I walked to the next house were Melissa was waiting with her two children.

"You look a lot better."

"It is a great day."

"Daddy home."

Melissa looked at me shocked but I just shook my head and nodded to Alex. Understanding she said nothing and we walked the children to school. Dropping the children off with their fellow class mates Melissa and I happily walked off. When we were far enough away she let rip.

"So how was it?"

"How was what?"

"You know."

"Oh um we didn't."

"WHAT? How come?"

"Alex attacked Lachlan."

"Oh yeah I can see how that would put a damper on things."

"Yeah it's one day at a time he's not leaving so that may help."

"Is there anything I can do?"

"No Mel but thank you this is a family thing not a pack thing."

"Well you know where I am."

"Thanks honey but I'm going to get some sleep before I have to pick the kids up."

"Alright I'll see you this afternoon."

"Sure."

Hugging Mel I went into my house and close the door. Part of me wished Lachlan would show up but I knew he was observing the kids. It was after all his job not as a father but the supreme alpha.

Going to my room I lay down and surprisingly fell asleep instantly. There was no grief and no nightmares. Several hours later a rapid knock came at my door. Thinking something was wrong I hurried to answer it.

"You haven't been asleep this whole time have you?"

"Why what time is it?"

"It's time to go get the kids."

"Oh shit lets go." Mel shook her head laughing at me.

"What's so funny?"

"I was sure you were getting laid but I could hear you snoring your head off."

"I wish."

And we both giggled. Getting to the school all four children came running up to us with their teacher who looked a little concerned. Giving the kids plenty of cuddles and kisses I then asked Melissa to head off without me. Looking concerned I shook my head and said I would follow soon. When they were far enough away the teacher finally spoke.

"There were a few incidents today."

"Oh no what happened?"

"Alex and Michael nearly ended up in a confrontation with a few other children."

"How bad was it?"

"Just know Alex is okay but he was bitten several times."

"Oh why?"

"His beta went to check on his younger brother so Alex went to play with the other children. Everything seemed fine but then Alex cried out. His beta came rushing over but we managed to defuse the situation before there was a huge problem."

"Well was the child at least punished?"

"His parents have been notified."

"Right and if it happens again?"

"One of the elder alphas was here and said he would take the incident to the council."

It had to be Lachlan I could only imagine what he felt within the moment and it actually made me smile.

"Don't stress I'm sure it was kids being kids they're bound to fight and play up."

I shook the teachers hand and walked off. I was super proud of my boy for not fighting and I was super proud of the dad to be for not stepping in.

When I got home all the children were in pup form in the pens learning to work as a team.

This wasn't working out too well as they were still kids, though their wolves were mature they allowed the behavior. I go to sit beside Melissa and lean my head on her shoulder.

"Hey are you alright?"

"Yes but I don't think my boy is."

"What do you mean?"

I told her about the incident at the school and Mel ended up rolling around in a fit of laughter.

"This isn't funny."

"Oh it's hilarious I could only imagine what Lachlan was thinking of doing."

"Yes but taking it to the council that's a bit much I mean kids are going to fight."
"Yes but think of it this way he may be trying to get into Alex's good books."
Seeing things from her point of view I couldn't help but smile and looking at my son he seemed to be in a better mood then yesterday. We sat side by side and watched the children roll around. In the end we just laughed and ushered them inside.
There was going to be no training today and that was fine by me I needed to check to make sure Alex was okay.
When the kids were in the house they ran to their rooms and came out fully dressed. I turned cartoons on and went about asking how there day was. My daughter squealed excitedly stating that she saw daddy. I waited for a growl or any sign that Alex was upset however he just kept watching TV.
When dinner was ready we all sat down to eat and that's when Alex told me he was bitten. I asked if he was okay and what happened. He said he was playing trains and a boy didn't want to share and bit him. He counted with his fingers four times. I felt sad for my boy and told him what the teacher said and that's when he said daddy said it would be okay. I was shell shocked but didn't push the subject.

Afterward it was bath and then bed.
Knowing it was going to take my girl a
while to settle I knock and walk into Alex's
room. He was already tucked up in bed.
"Do you need me to tuck you in?"
"No, where is daddy?"
"I don't know buddy, I'm sure he's around."
"Did he go again?"
"What, no baby no, he's here to stay."
"I want daddy."
"I know baby I know me too."
Out of bloody nowhere Lachlan appeared.
Alex jumped out of bed and flew into
Lachlan's arms. Trying not to cry I left the
boys to their bonding and went to check on
my girl.
Knocking on her door I found her asleep
upside down in bed. Picking her up I placed
her right side up and put the covers over her.
Walking out quietly I could hear the boys
whispering. Standing at the door I could
hear Lachlan telling Alex about the
kidnapping and why he had no choice but to
leave. There were many sniffles and many
whys and why nots but I heard Lachlan
doing the best he could.
Walking out to the lounge room I waited for
Lachlan to join me but I eventually fell
asleep. Waking up in shock several hours
later I checked on my daughter and she was
fine.I go to check on Alex and to my

surprise Lachlan was still in there and was fast asleep. Alex ended up drawing my attention. He was growling and whimpering in his sleep. I open the pack bond and sure enough he was in fact asleep it was his wolf causing the commotion.

"Sir is everything alright?"

"You know what your mate did?"

"No what?"

"He promised my boy to never leave again?"

"Isn't that a good thing?"

"No as he may just have too."

"And together we'll deal with it, we'll get him ready in advance."

"And what if he has to do it suddenly?"

"I don't know. I see your point and will talk about it with Lachlan but for now rest Alpha you're causing Alex distress."

He growled but agreed. I felt for my little alpha. Stuck with a wolf the age of a teenager but the mind and body of a four year old. Wiping my hand over the faces of both my son and mate I smiled and went to bed.

The next day I woke and found it was almost lunch time. Walking out of my room both Lachlan and the children were gone. Freaking out I went rushing outside and nearly crashed into Melissa.

"Hey slow down where's the fire?"

"THERE GONE THERE ALL GONE."
"Hey, hey come here they're fine."
"Well where are they?"
"There out in the territory somewhere."
"WHAT, WHY."
"Shhh… come inside and I'll tell you."
Growling I marched inside and sat on the
lounge. Melissa looked ready to bolt but
stood her ground.
"So Lachlan woke with the kids however
Alex's wolf was playing up."
"Yeah I know Alpha was pissed last night."
"Well to help the young pup he took all the
children out to hunt and play hide and seek."
"In the whole territory?"
"Yes and before you flip out anyone over
the age of eighteen has been asked to babysit
all the children."
"Oh and that should make me happy?"
"You should the dragon queen herself has
your pups and from what I heard they are
winning."
I didn't know if I should still be pissed or
friggen proud that my kids were out
matching their father. Trying not to freak out
I spent the day getting massages and
shopping.
By the end of the day I had finally managed
to relax. Heading home I was greeted by the
queen and Lachlan each had a sleepy child
in their arms.

181

Hurrying forward I unlocked the door and allowed everyone to place the children in their beds. When they came out both were smiling and talking about a meeting they needed to attend.

Casey rushed forward in my mind taking control of my body. I thought she would have been happy to see our mate instead she slapped him clean across the face.

Chapter Fourteen

Lachlan

She slapped me I couldn't believe she slapped me. The queen giggled beside me and disappeared leaving the conversation unfinished. Cade was snickering inside my mind.

"I told you she would be pissed."

"Shut up."

I looked towards Amanda but she walked away. Man oh man I was in the dog house. She went and sat on the lounge looking quite shocked herself.

I went to sit on the other lounge and just waited for her to explain. After a while she spoke but she broke down crying.

"I'm sorry I'm so, so sorry."

I leaped out of the chair and went to her. Picking her up I sat on the lounge with her on my lap. I allowed her to cry it out.

In that moment I felt like a complete dick of a mate. I should have woke her up and told her what I was doing. After a while she finally stopped crying and just quietly sat there.

"What is going to happen to me?"

"What do you mean?"

"I struck you in front of the queen no less."

"Oh nothing she probably thought I had it coming." I smiled down at her.

"I know this doesn't change what happened but it was Casey she, she just took total control she was so angry."

"It's alright Cade said it was a bad idea."

"For me it ended up being okay but I guess Casey..."

"I know I have some grovelling to do and I will tomorrow for now let's go to bed it's been a long couple of days."

Kissing the top of her head I carried her to our room where I put her down and proceed to pull the covers back. She stripped down to just her underwear and got under the covers. Looking at me longingly I quickly stripped down to my boxes and jumped in beside her.

She snuggled into me kissing my cheek, before long little snores filled my ears. Slowly but surely I fell asleep with a smile on my face. It was the best sleep of my life until I was awoken by two screaming toddlers.

Opening my eyes both children were bouncing all over me and the bed. Grabbing my daughter mid bounce I tickle the life out of her. Alex yelled he wanted a turned so he got exactly what he asked for.

"Alright, alright come on you guys have school come on."

"But muuuuum."

"No buts come on you got to see daddy let's go."

With a groan from Alex and some tears from Lily both kids left. I lay back down in bed with my arms above my head. This was living the dream. A mate who loved me and two cute little terrors in my arms each and every day life was good.

I nearly fell asleep when I remembered the meeting with the council. Quickly getting dressed I ran out the door.

On the way a sudden idea came into my mind but I had to get the packs help. Sending an SOS to both Melissa, her mate and Amanda's parents I walked into the meeting with my head held high.

Smiling at my new soon to be friends and bowing to the thrones I found a seat and sat down. Everyone went through each species problems like land development, housing, pack fights etc., it was quite boring. When it was almost time for things to end the queen stood causing a ruckus.

"Attention, attention, yesterday I got invited by mere passing to a rather unique training session. As I only watched some of what was going on I want our new council member to explain what it was he did."

All heads turned towards me some looked pissed while others looked amused. Making

my way to the front of the room I stood next
to the queen and addressed the room.

"As you know I had to step away from my
family for two years. Within this time you
got to know my mate and watch her raise
our children alone."

Some of the members mumbled an
agreement but they were shut down by the
queen.

"Shush now… continue please Lachlan."

"What you may not know is the affect this
had on my mate and our son. My mate
withdrew from the pack, her wolf refused to
change and she was always in grief.

Our children were the only thing keeping
her going. When I returned I didn't know
what to expect but what I got was an angry
greater alpha pup with abandonment issues.
The first day we met he tried to attack me. I
eventually allowed him to in the hopes to
calm him.

This however didn't work. I went to the
school the next day just to watch the
children and in the end nearly kicking one of
your little shits arse. Do not worry no child
was harmed but boy did I want to.

Anyway the teacher allowed me to talk to
my son and I promised him I would deal
with it. No, this is not a council matter but I
said I'd bring it to you all the same."

"Get to the point."

"So anyway family drama aside I decided to reconnect with my children and help my son by creating a training excuse. What we normally teach children is defense and offense, tracking and marking but what we don't teach them is hide and seek."

"You've got to be joking he's talking about a game children play."

"Shush now let him finish."

"Thank you your highness. Anyway as I said hide and seek. It was the seeking part that was important, they had to find their pack mates without using their wolf. The younger children preferred to actually play hide and seek however the oldest of the lot found the exercise quite enthralling.

I had different council members and their children watching over the wolf pack while the children sorted out their friends.

With different smells and types of animals around the children had no choice but to track, listen and observe. In the end my two children won however winning was not the point.

It was a training exercise to not rely on our wolves. With the queens help I got my children home safe and sound but was soon after slapped by my mate."

This time laughter went around the room and this time I joined them.

"So does anyone here know what the training exercise was really about?"
Everyone sat quietly looking confused and a little annoyed.
"What Lachlan tried to do was teach the children that they can't always rely on their wolf and pack. In Lachlan's case it had a different meaning but the same outcome."
Nodding my head I watched as a few people raised their hands.
"Why do we need to know this?"
"Because as soon as a greater alpha is born to your species you must go out and train them."
"Don't we all have to rule on this?"
"Not this time the king's word is final."
Everyone looked towards his royal highness but he agreed with his queen. Chatter broke out throughout the room and I knew it was my time to leave. Going outside I was greeted by my son's pack members.
"What will it be alpha?"
"I need your help Amanda and I need no crave time alone.
Now the children are okay I think we can leave them with one of you for the night.
"Us! They can stay with us. I'm the closest thing to smelling like Amanda being her mother and all."
"Right thank you I owe you."

"No need just look after our girl and those grandbabies."

"Oh I plan to, I need help getting Amanda away from the house. I have to go to the shops, do dinner and set up. You know get the mood going."

"I got it I have an ultrasound to get to but I can say Simon needed to help you."

"Great idea."

"Sure then we can go for pickles and ice cream."

Lucky I was a fully grown wolf because the sound of that made me want to gag.

"I'm joking alpha although Amanda did crave that during her pregnancy so you're screwed."

I must have turned white or something because everyone looked at me and laughed. Everyone took off at different directions leaving me looking the fool. I knew we missed our mate but that had to be the golden rule for tonight NO BITING.

Shaking it of the best I could I made my way into the nearest town.

I brought all the roses I could and a massive pork roast. Grabbing wine and the rest of the pieces I needed I was about to head off when Melissa for some strange reason sent me the measurements for some skimpy clothing.

Unsure what to do with it I walked into several clothing stores before I figured out what it was I was meant to be buying. If I hadn't been around so many people my cock would have been rock hard. Amanda would look amazing in all of them.

Looking at several I eventually found a black two piece.

Practically drooling as my memory went to that black dress she wore the night we made love. Finally managing to get out of there I took off for home.

Nearly breaking the speed limit I made it in plenty of time to put the roast on, have a shower and completely set up the house for a romantic evening.

When Amanda finally arrived home she was laughing and smiling as she walked in the door. When she looked at me and then the house she dropped all her bags. A hand flew straight to mouth.

"Surprise."

"Where are the children?"

"They're with your parents don't worry I've been told on good authority they're having the time of their lives."

She walked into the house and looked around. I tried to see it from her eyes however I was shit scared that I had gone over bored. She went into the kitchen and opened the oven. Closing her eyes she took in a big whiff. Standing back up she turned towards me and the look made me want to fuck her on the kitchen counter.

She stepped towards me however I stepped back.

She looked at me confused for a second however that look was back. I explained that a bath awaited her and there was some clothing on the bed for her to wear. I could see she was so conflicted. The mum in her knew the bath sounded really good but the wolf in her was going mental I bet. She eventually made the choice to walk out of the room.

Taking a deep breath I tried to reign in my own wolf. I kept myself busy ensuring dinner was ready and the wine was nicely chilled. After half an hour an

"OH MY GOD" filled the house.

She had managed to get to the bedroom. I didn't know if it was the setting or the clothes but I was soon to find out. After several painstakingly moments her voice came from around the corner and I stood up.

"I look ridiculous."

"I'm sure you look fine."

"I haven't worn something like this in years."

"I would hope not but if it makes you feel better it was Melissa's idea."

"I'm going to kill her."

191

"I hope not the children won't be pleased."
A shy giggle greeted my ears and then out
stepped Amanda. If my jaw could hit the
floor it would have she looked completely
stunning. Though the outfit was very see
through it fit her perfectly.
It enhanced every curve while hiding any
women's dreaded flaws. The image of her
like this was going to be burnt in my mind
forever.
She shyly looked at the ground but my wolf
opened the mating bond wide open and she
felt everything we were feeling.
"OH my."
"Indeed come eat, I made your favorite."
"How did you know let me guess…"
"Yes Melissa. Now come, come eat or we
won't make it through dinner."
Sending out a cheap shot Casey sent us an
image of us making love. By god poor Cade
went ballistic. Growling out loud it was met
by a shy giggle from Amanda. I stepped
toward her chair and then waited for her to
sit down.
When she did I grabbed everything from the
kitchen and hurried to sit down.
We managed to get through an uneventful
meal. She did her mummy thing excusing
herself from the table to ring and check on
the kids but she was back in seconds.
"Is everything alright?"

"Everything is amazing."

"You haven't seen anything yet."

"Oh really."

Smiling at her I got up and went to the lounge room where I set up the fireplace and went and got another bottle of wine. While doing so she was watching my every move almost stalking me.

Ignoring her the best I could I went back for the dessert and then held out my hand for her to hold. Taking it she allowed me to escort her to the lounge room where we both laid down.

Enjoying the warmth and each other's company we kept the conversation light but in reality we were a ticking time bomb. When dessert was finished we snuggled together just enjoying the moment.

"Do you hear that?"

"Hear what?"

"Exactly I haven't had this kind of peace since before Alex was born."

"I can't promise our lives will be like this always but I will at least try."

"Try is all we can do when we have children."

She rolled over and planted a kiss on my lips. Her embrace was the queue my wolf needed to let loose. Devouring her mouth I deepened the kiss. She moaned into my mouth causing a growl from me. At this

point I was more wolf than man. I stood up
scooping her from the floor and charged into
our bedroom. Throwing her on the bed I
quickly ripped my clothes off and pounced
on her.

Not giving her a chance to get comfortable I
ripped the clothing from her body.

"Hey I thought you like that?"

"I got you another."

Spreading her legs I felt to see if she was
wet. To Cade's delight she was. I positioned
myself and thrusted forward Amanda yelled
out. Stopping for a split second I looked at
her. S

he nodded her head and held onto my arms.
I wanted this second time to be as magical
as the first but Cade wouldn't allow it. With
Amanda screaming for more I pounded into
her with everything I had.

Before long her orgasm built and I just
exploded inside her. Without thinking I
leaned down and bit into her shoulder
causing us both to go over the edge again.
Both of us breathing heavily I looked down
at my mate. She was completely sated from
the high.

Leaning down I kiss her and roll off. We lie
quietly for a moment neither of us having
anything to say when suddenly.

"Shit, shit, shit I am so sorry, I am so, so sorry. This is not how I wanted the night to end."

"Is it over already?" she cheekily smiled at me.

"Yes I mean no, I don't know."

I placed an arm over myself completely ashamed.

"Hey talk to me."

"You're going to be pregnant again."

"So?"

"I wanted to wait to prove myself."

"You're not leaving anytime soon are you?"

"Not that I know of."

"Then let's just be here, now just us as tomorrow we will have two little terrors to deal with."

"You're right I'm sorry I wrecked the mood."

"Oh baby we're just getting started."

She climbed on top of me and showed me just how much she loved me. It wasn't until dawn the next day that we finally fell asleep in each other's arms.

Epilogue

After our romantic night together Lachlan was true to his word. He managed to convince the council to allow him to hang around for the pregnancy. It was amazing and horrifying.

The mood swings, the cravings, poor Lachlan ended up with constant heartburn and vomiting. The children hadn't helped matters. When I yelled they would transform and run around the house like headless chooks.

Then there was the toe to toe between Alex and Lachlan when I would randomly cry. It was no one's fault it was all the hormones. Over the years Lachlan learned to control his wolf however we did end up with two more children along the way.

Luckily none of them were alphas but we still had our troubles all the same. Each of the children chose their alpha and again popped into pups.

There was constant fighting, yelling and screaming, add in the hunting and we were your normal typical pack. Just over run and being run by children.

Poor Melissa had it a lot harder than us as she ended up with a tribe of pups. Every time I congratulated her but deep down I was secretly grateful. After the last pregnancy I even offered to buy Cade a muzzle, he was none too impressed.

Lachlan did leave us now and again but always came back and the children got used to their dad being mister boss man. Sometimes Alex's abandonment issues would rise but the boys would dish it out, go hunting or just plain yell at each other until they finally got over it. All our children deep down loved their father. I also loved him as well. When he was home he was an amazing dad and mate.

On the day of Alex's eighteenth birthday a big celebration was held. Not only was he a man but he officially was to go and live with the remaining greater alpha. This was a joyful day but also heart breaking. My mind constantly wandering to the early days. When he was my little alpha forcing me to change, making Casey do stupid and funny things.

"Hey mum are you okay."

"I am but we need to have a chat come with me."

I walked us away from the group and found a nice quiet area to sit. Holding his hand I looked deep into his eyes. As tears fell silently down my face I renounced my claim to his pack.

When I was done several howls broke out through the clearing, my family and our friends were already prepared. The disconnection hurt all the same. Soon a lot of them would be leaving with Alex.

My son grabbed me in a huge bear hug and held me tight. I cried on his shoulder until I had nothing left to give.

"It's alright mum I understand you need to be here with dad."

"I know baby but to me you will forever be my little alpha."

We held each other tight until Lachlan came to find us. Come on you two enough tears there's a party over here. All of us laughing Lachlan reached out his hands and helped us up off the ground. Holding his son in a bear hug he patted his back and sent him on his way.

"You couldn't have waited until tomorrow."

"No because today was the day he stopped being a little alpha and becomes the man and greater wolf we raised him to be."

Hand in hand we made our way back to the celebrations and onto a brand new future. Hell motherhood wasn't over yet, one I still had to deal with my youngest children and two my daughter dating Melissa's son which was really sending Lachlan around the twist.

Author Notes

When I first started this book I had no title
or origin story. All I had was a built book
and a couple of lines. As the months went on
the book really wasn't going anywhere until
an idea came to mind.

You see my toddler is a special needs child,
mentally speaking he has issues which need
to be explored. Really thinking of him the
title came to life and then the story soon
followed.

My toddler is a handful in his own way just
as little alpha was. They're both so alike I
had so much fun actually assessing my
child's personally.

My toddler is very smart, hyperactive,
stubborn and a head strong child. We have
daily challenges but I cannot see my life
without him.

Getting inside the mind of this female was
easy enough as I have been in her shoes. It is
hard raising a child or children on your own.
It is more challenging when they have
special needs. This story really allowed me
to explore my mind and find the trying parts
of parenthood but also the fun side.

As for the relationship between the female
and male leads this allowed me to really
look at their relationship and also assess my
own.

This book took me on one epic adventure that I was actually really sad to see finish. If you managed to make it to the end of my story I want to thank you from the bottom of my heart. This book gave me all the feels and I hope it did for you to.

Please write a review it will only take one minute.

Otherwise you can follow me on Tiktok (Krissiephillips89), Instagram (krissiephillips4) or Facebook (Krissie Phillips). I do have twitter however I just use that to chat to like-minded readers, writers and authors.

P.s for all the single mothers/fathers out there allow yourself to have your bad days, with every bad day comes a new shiny one. When those good days come around really enjoy them because you never know what the next one will bring.

One last piece of advice, never live just for your child it can become toxic and unhealthy. Both you and your child need room to socialize, have hobbies and just live. It is okay to let go because nine times out of ten they're going to come back home.

About the Author

Krissie is an Australian author who started writing in her early teens. Simple poems at first to see if she could get the creative juices flowing. As she got older, she realized her life story which was one of many twists and turns.

Releasing her first book in 2019 Krissie had come to realize just how much she loved to write. So, with that she released another and another. She has many more stories to share with the world but she's slow on the down time.

Krissie is a mother of three beautiful children and also a proof reader on the side. Her career is supported by her wonderful partner who helps her any way he can. Though Krissie's life is full on sometimes she does try and make time for her fans and loves chatting about anything book related. Other than that, Krissie is a pretty quiet person who loves the simple things in life, like hanging out with her partner and family. On a Friday night they all relax and just talk about nothing and listen to music. She also plays video games and colors in, in her down time and going for walks with her toddler. If you like her stories please leave her reviews. Thank you.

Other books released by Krissie Phillips

Forgiven: - An Autobiography Released
May 2019
Fantasy Provider: - An Erotic Fantasy
Released August 2019
The Lost Phoenix: - Harem/Paranormal
Romance Released February 2020
The Devamp's journey: - Paranormal
Romance Released April 2020
The Great Witch: - Reverse Harem Released
July 2020
Cowboy's 4 Me: - Reverse Harem Released
December 2020

Up and coming
Forbidden coven – Reverse Harem

Made in the USA
Monee, IL
12 September 2021

77845850R00115